MYSTERY OF THE MEDALLION

Jeff Edwards

InterSkillMedia.com

This novel is a work of fiction. The characters, names, dates, incidents, dialogue, and plot are the products of the author's imagination or used fictitiously.

To purchase other titles or to purchase the audio version of this title, please visit, www.InterSkillMedia.com

ISBN 10: 0-9820797-3-7

ISBN 13: 978-0-9820797-3-7

Made in The United States of America

www.InterSkillMedia.com

Made in The United States of America

Dedication

This story would never have been told without the inspiration of Brett Staggs and L.A. 'Chip' Hoyt. In a small conference room, an idea was hatched to help boost the music and song writing career of one talented Pennsylvania native and Austin, Texas transplant, Brett Staggs. During a brainstorming session, someone came up with a story-line involving James Dean and the legendary story of his famous race car, the Porsche 550 Spyder.

While the tale begins with the fateful crash, the real story is about a very artistic musician, his incredible song writing skills and how a small group of people came together to make this story come alive.

The music, written and performed by Brett Staggs for the original Audio Movie is soulful and inspirational. As many have stated after listening to his music, "I can't stop listening to it!"

The story line and editing process would never have been completed without the efforts of L.A. 'Chip' Hoyt. He is an excellent storyteller, a masterful screenwriter and a skillful editor who knows why good stories happen. Like a kid on an amusement ride, it was a fun and enjoyable experience to meet him every day and explore what direction this story would eventually travel. Without his character development and editing guidance, the original Audio

3

Movie would never have seen the light of day.

The script began with an Audio Movie in mind. Much like the old Radio Dramas of the 1930's and 1940's, the Audio Movie, more than two hours in length, brings the characters to life. It is one thing to read the story, it is another experience altogether to actually hear all the characters come off the page and into the theater of the mind.

Casting for the Audio Movie was easy. Austin, Texas has a large base of talented actors whose voices made the Audio Movie much more than an audio book. These actors not only have voiceover talent, they are actors in every sense of the word. Beginning with Amy Staggs, the wife of Brett Staggs and a very talented actor in her own right, she made her character more than real. Shane Wells played the younger Brett Staggs and was excellent. Michael Dalmon played Marty Staggs and was incredible. He *was* Marty Staggs. He made everyone laugh. John McLean played the Sheriff, J.P. Smith and made the character authentic. His voice is unlike any other. Shirley Price played the women in Memphis and did a great job. She is a real sport and is an actor if I ever saw one. Chris Patton, the man of many voices helped to make the Audio Movie like no other audio book ever recorded. There are many more fine actors, Jake S. Krane, Paul McGinty Dan'l Terry, Kem Hughes Edwards, David Volk, Cindy Macomber, Randy Kelly, Robert Sliger, Randi Potenzo, and Pepper Daniel who all made the Audio Movie a fun and interesting story.

What audio book has anyone ever listened to that included more than thirty voices?

Each and every one of the actors mentioned did not simply read their lines, their acting skills, more than just voiceover talent, made each scene believable. To this I applaud them all.

Originally, the title of the Audio Movie was 'Curse of The Little Bastard'. You will need to read the entire book to understand that particular title. However, after hearing too many objections, the title was changed.

The book actually came much later than the Audio Movie. Taking the manuscript that was used to record the Audio Movie, the story needed more depth and the process of converting a script written for audio to a novel began.

Finally, take a few minutes to check out the music of Brett Staggs whether on Itunes or InterSkillMedia.com. His music will inspire you.

Jeff Edwards

Chapter One

Deep in the heart of Los Angeles in a Hollywood studio, a very small group of sound engineers and actors watched rushes of a just completed major motion picture.

The dark room was filled with a thick cloud as nearly everyone smoked.

The Director sat behind a desk by the controls and hadn't spoken a word since the projector had started nearly an hour before. No one was sure what he thought about the images on the screen. Silence usually meant something was terribly wrong.

The movie had been filmed in the small West Texas town of Marfa and after months of back breaking work, the film was finished and ready for editing.

The projector room was dark when suddenly the phone rang. The screen came to a halt, freezing the picture. Lights went up. Everyone turned and looked at him, telephone dangling in his hand. The Director looked like he had seen a ghost, his skin had changed colors right before their eyes. Slowly he stood up, his voice coming from a place far away when he said, "There's been a car crash. James Dean has been killed".

Several hundred miles away, a mangled 1955 Porsche Spyder was hoisted onto a flatbed truck while workers gathered smaller pieces of the vehicle's remains, a headlight here, a door hinge there.

Little did they know, a part of the car was now missing.

Someone had taken a piece of the James Dean Porsche Spyder and then suddenly disappeared...

Chapter Two

I was raised on a farm in central Pennsylvania and by the time I turned sixteen I knew turning up dirt was not to be my life's work.

It's not that I didn't like working hard. I guess if I were to put my finger on it, I'd have to say it was getting up at four in the morning and going to bed when the sun set.

My brother Jim, on the other hand, liked to farm. He was the first one up in the morning and the last one back from the field. He thought I was just plain lazy but that is the furthest thing from the truth.

The way I've always seen it, some people were meant to be doctors, some were meant to be lawyers and some, god help them, were meant to be politicians.

Me, I wasn't meant to be any of those things. I remember the day I made up my mind what I really wanted to do. I was looking at the newspaper and I read about a place called Hollywood and what was happening there, I thought at the time, well, it sounded pretty exciting.

So, when I was old enough to leave home, I said goodbye to my family and friends.

My Mom, bless her sweet heart, she cried and my Dad just shook my hand and said what I thought he would say. Just don't get into any trouble.

They didn't want me to leave but, I told them I just had to. They never understood that it was the music I was following and if I was to ever to make it, I knew it wouldn't happen in a small town. At least not the one I was from.

So, on a cold autumn morning, I climbed on the bus and headed west.

* * * * * *

ON A CALIFORNIA HIGHWAY, a few hours north of Los Angeles, a 1955 Ford station wagon rolled along. Its two occupants, Bill Hickman and Sanford Roth were following the famous actor, James Dean who was more than anxious to race his 1955 Porsche Spyder at the Salinas Airport.

Bill was frustrated. He had lost sight of Dean's silver race car more than thirty minutes before. "Why does he have to drive so fast?" He looked over at Sanford who was reading a Life magazine. "I can't see the Porsche anymore."

"It's an engine with four wheels. What do you expect?" Sanford replied.

"I told him I didn't mind driving the station wagon. But, I didn't expect him to leave us behind!"

"Look. You'd do the same if it were your racecar."

Bill gripped the steering wheel hard. He was the teacher, not the student. The fact that the young actor took off was like a kid cutting class. "Just because his name is James Dean and he's made three movies everybody thinks he's God."

Sanford was more laid back. He didn't think it was really a big deal. "Well, after Giant, everybody needed a break. He's still a kid, cut him some slack. Speaking of breaks, there's a gas station up ahead. I could use something to drink."

Bill looked at his watch and shook his head. "San, if we stop, he'll start the race without us." Bill said.

"Come on, it'll only take five minutes and besides, we can ask if there's a short cut to Salinas."

"Alright, make it quick. But, I doubt there's a short cut."

Stopping for something to drink and directions, the two men got out and walked toward the gas station.

Under the aluminum porch, a young man was sitting in a chair. By his side, a Silvertone Guitar leaned against the wall. Taking a long drag from a

Chesterfield King, he studied a map of California.

Inside, the two men pulled glass soda bottles out of a coke machine. The crusty old man behind the counter struggled to tune his radio.

"Blasted thing. They don't make 'em like they used to." He said.

Impatient, Bill cleared his throat.

"Help you fellas?" Looking up, the old man saw two soda bottles. "Oh, that'll be 10 cents."

"How far to Salinas?" Bill asked.

The old man looked at Sanford then, back at Bill. He wasn't sure who they were or what they would be doing once they got there. Sensing no immediate danger, he tried to help.

"Salinas? I'd say two, maybe three hours. Depends on what you're driving."

That was not what Bill wanted to hear and simply repeated what he had heard for no particular reason. "Three hours, huh?

"Well, if you can go as fast as that streakin bullet that came by here a while ago, shoot, you'd get there in a heartbeat!"

Bill knew he was referring to the Porsche and just hearing the old man say it only made it worse. "Damn! Are there any shortcuts?"

"Nope, just stay on 466 till you get to Paso Robles, then head north." The old man said as he put the two nickels in the cash register.

"Thanks." Bill said.

"Glad I could help. Come back anytime."

As Bill and Sanford walked out, the old man picked up a hammer. "Blasted radio, probably made in Japan."

Outside, Bill and San studied the young man who had not moved an inch.

"Hey friend, mind if we take a look at your map?" Bill asked.

The young man looked up at Bill and Sanford, then over at the station wagon. "Sure, on one condition." He said.

"Yea, what's that?"

"I could use a ride."

"Where you headed?" Bill asked.

"San Francisco. I got an uncle there. I thought I'd see him before I hit L.A."

"How about Salinas?" Bill offered.

"Sure."

As the three climbed into the car, Sanford spoke up.

"What's your name?"

"I go by Garrett, Garrett Arizona."

"Well, Garrett, you any good with that guitar?"

"Well, I usually play for money."

It was a beautiful September day in California when Bill Hickman, Sanford Roth and Garrett Arizona drove north in pursuit of James Dean and his race car.

In less than an hour, they came upon the accident. The 1955 Porsche was mangled beyond recognition. He was still alive when Bill found him. Sadly, within minutes, James Dean died in his arms.

It was only a matter of hours when Hollywood learned they had lost one of their own. For Bill and Sanford, they had lost a true friend. To Garrett Arizona, he knew very little of James Dean. Standing next to the wrecked car, he found a shiny piece of metal with an emblem and put it in his pocket.

After the accident, the mangled sports car was bought by its designer for $2,500 dollars. His name was Chuck Barris, creator of the famous Bat Mobile. Upon arrival to the Barris' garage, the car fell on a mechanic, breaking both legs.

Not long after, Barris sold the engine and tires to two race car drivers. One died and the other was seriously injured with the car's engine and tires aboard.

Later, while trying to steal the car's steering wheel, a young teen severely gashed his arm.

Then, a man who purchased the remaining tires was involved in an auto accident of his own. The two tires, coincidentally, blew out at the same time.

Barris offered the car to the California Highway Patrol who wanted to display the wrecked car at various High Schools to demonstrate auto safety.

Soon after, the garage housing the car burned to the ground and every vehicle inside was destroyed, except one.

Later on, a man hauling the car on a flatbed truck was killed instantly when it rolled on top of him.

After only a few short years, Barris had had enough. He loaded the wrecked car on a train headed back to California.

When it arrived, the car was nowhere to be found and hasn't been seen since.

Chapter Three

I remember the crash scene like it was ten minutes ago. I don't think I'll ever forget it.

I was sitting in the back of the station wagon talking to San who was in the front seat. Bill was driving. He didn't say much. San said he was mad that Jimmy Dean took off and left them behind.

Anyway, we pulled off the side of the road and got out. It was an ugly scene.

The Ford Coupe that Dean slammed into was in the middle of the road, while the young man driving it was sitting in his car, dazed.

The race car had been crushed like a tin can. Someone, I don't remember who, said it was a Porsche. It sure didn't look like one.

Bill and San went over to Dean who was still in the car. Except for that one day, I don't think I've ever seen a grown man cry. Bill sure did.

The other person in the car with Dean was his mechanic. He looked pretty bad but, he made it. I heard he later got killed in a car crash, which to me was very strange. Most people go through life and never get in a car crash and this man is in two and the second one

*killed him. Maybe he should have taken
a bus.*

*What amazed me was the fact that there
were pieces of automobile parts
everywhere. The road was littered with
glass, chunks of metal, I even found
someone's shoe.*

*Lying in the middle of the road was
the insignia from the hood of the race
car. I don't know why I decided to keep
it.*

*At the time, it seemed like the right
thing to do.*

* * * * * *

FIFTY YEARS LATER, wearing only a pair
of jeans and a tee shirt, Brett Staggs
rifled through the laundry looking for
a clean pair of socks.

Every morning was the same. Wait to
the last minute and then panic when he
couldn't find what he was looking for.

At 19, Brett was happy. He was about
to graduate. He loved music and had
worked hard, very hard, to learn the
guitar. Now he was part of a band.

Playing music had given him something
few other things could. An identity
perhaps. He simply loved music and in a
short time, he had become the lead
singer and guitar player for a popular

16

local band. It was now his band. His voice and songwriting had brought the band from an opening act a year before to the featured act in high school dances across five counties.

He had a vision of where his music could take them. A career path that would lead to the top of the charts. His fellow band members loved the idea of becoming famous, but none of them shared the understanding of the many steps it would take to get there.

On this particular morning in late May, Brett headed off to practice for the local high school prom. Brett had a couple of new songs and to say he was excited was an understatement.

Brett had a plan for everything including the color of sox he wore each day of the week. It was a constant source of annoyance that his Mom always demanded that he follow her plans to the letter but, never paid any attention to his.

At the moment, that didn't matter, if he couldn't find what he was looking for, he'd be late for sure.

Brett yelled from another room. "Mom, have you seen my black socks? This is black sock day."

"I told you last night they're in the hamper. You've got plenty of white ones. And, Brett, eat something before you go. Oatmeal or toast?"

"I gotta go! I'm picking Amy up. She wants to hear us practice."

"Brett, I know you have big plans to be the next Elvis, but, honey, you need to eat. You know what happens when your blood sugar falls."

"Mom! I have no desire to be Elvis. And, stop talking about blood sugar. I'm not a kid anymore!"

"Honey, that's what Mom's do. Worry about blood sugar. So, before your next world tour, you need to…"

"Have you seen my harmonica?" Brett asked.

"I put it with your sheet music in the attic."

"Mom. Stop moving my stuff!" He said.

"Brett. I put it where it belongs. You can't leave things lying around. It's called organization." She reminded him one more time.

"Alright, but please stop moving my stuff."

"Ok. You start putting your stuff where it belongs and I'll stop moving it."

Annoyed, Brett made his way to the attic. It was more like a sanctuary than anything.

Above the two car garage, the attic was a quiet place where he could be completely alone to write music and play his guitar. Five years before, his father had built it just before he died. On one side he kept his equipment, a guitar stand, drum set, speakers, and microphones. It also had a window that remained a true and loyal friend. It welcomed warm sunlight when winter was beginning to break and in the hot summer, you could raise it six inches and a cool breeze would find its way through.

Looking out, he could just about see the entire farm.

It wasn't much to look at now. With his father gone, there was no one to work the land. A farmer Brett was not. Now, he had bigger plans.

On the far corner of the room, Sue Staggs kept a wardrobe which also served as a museum of her late husband. It was very organized with a place for everything and everything in its place. She wasn't able, just yet, to get rid of his things. The fact was, she couldn't bring herself to the reality that he wasn't coming back. He had died in a fiery car accident. The police wouldn't allow her to see him. It was bad. After the funeral, she rarely left the house. Soon, depression set in and she slept constantly. But, after a month, the necessities of motherhood had pulled her out of that cold dark place. A long string of tragedies had cast a dark shadow over her family's history and by god she wasn't about to let her son grow up without her protecting him.

As Brett reached the top of the stairs, he turned on the light and heard a voice from behind.

"Hey! Dude." Came the intruder.

"Jay, why do you always do that?"

"Do what?"

Jay Hawkins had been his best friend since the seventh grade when Jay's family had moved just down the road from Saddleback Farm. He wasn't the brightest candle in the cathedral but, Jay was likeable. He could get anyone to do anything for him. His mother would get him to return things to Win-Mart when she had lost the receipt. With a big smile, he would ask the cashier for his money back and get it.

Jay played the drums. He was good, very good. When the former lead singer had left for college the year before, Jay invited Brett to join the band. That was fine with Jay, he and Jude never could agree on anything. The songs, the tempo, you name it.

"Hey, you ready to go?" Jay asked.

"Yea, I just had to get my harmonica." Brett said.

"Say, I think we should do a road trip after graduation, you know, we could make it a party trip."

Jay loved to brainstorm. Everyone else called it dreaming. "You know Pittsburgh then, Chicago. I hear the

20

bands play at night then, party 'til the sun comes up."

"Jay, it's not about the parties. We have to get serious. If we make the right moves, we'll create our own world tour." Brett said.

"Now, that sounds like a party!"

As they both stood in the attic, Jay was impressed. "Man, your Mom really has some neat stuff up here."

"I don't think you're getting what I'm saying."

While Jay was thinking about parties, Brett had been considering non-stop what all they would have to do as a band to make it. From everyone in the business to all that he had read on his own, it was not going to be easy. Making music was one thing, getting lots of people to listen to it and turning it into a real livelihood was another thing altogether.

"Listen, if we're going to make it to the top of the charts, there's a lot we have to do in between."

Ignoring Brett's words of wisdom, Jay found an old trunk in a corner of the attic.

Other than the four inch brass straps that covered it, the trunk had originally been painted black. "Wow! What's this? Looks like a Civil War chest. Any gold in here?" Jay asked laughing out loud.

"Jay, leave it alone! Mom will get mad if she saw you. Besides, there's a lock on it."

Jay looked all around the trunk. "It looks like it's been in a train wreck. What's inside?"

"Jay, there's a lock on it." Brett said.

"I'm telling you, there's no lock!"

Opening the old trunk, it made a squeak and a groan that revealed years without ever being opened. Inside, the old trunk had been lined with red silk that was clearly showing its age. More than one hundred years before, the original owner had it specially made as a wedding gift back in San Francisco. Over the years, it had changed hands many times and now sat in silence. If only it could speak. What stories it could tell.

Peering inside, Jay looked as if he had found nothing less than hidden treasures. "Whoa! There's a lot of neat stuff in here. Look at this. It's a bra made with cones!"

"Jay, put that stuff back. If my Mom sees you, I'm the one that'll be in trouble."

"Hey, this stuff is old."

Jay pulled out a pile of faded letters. Their original color was white, but, they had faded over time. Now, they looked antique. The letters were addressed to Brett Staggs, Box 124, Saddleback farm, Williamsport, Pennsylvania.

Holding the letters in his hand, Jay was surprised they had never been opened.

"Hey, you never opened these letters."

"I'm telling you one last time to close the trunk!" Brett said in a tone that said one last warning.

"Alright. But, what are all these letters about?"

As Jay closed the trunk, the sound of a cell phone went off. Brett pulled his phone out of his bag and answered. "Hi Babe. You ready? Yea, I'll pick you up in twenty minutes. Ok... love you, too. Bye."

Brett stuffed the letters in his backpack along with his sheet music. He never expected to find letters addressed to him in his mother's trunk. But, he didn't dare open them anywhere near his Mom. There would be hell to pay if she found him snooping around her private things.

The two boys jumped in Brett's pickup and drove toward Williamsport. The truck was a 1980 version his Dad had given him on his seventeenth birthday. Other than the fact that the paint was fading, he liked being able to go anywhere without worrying about scratching it. He used it to haul hay to one of the back pastures to feed the horses when his Dad was still alive. The truck was one of the last of a dying breed of pickups before Mr. Plastic took over. He liked the truck because he thought it was rugid. Once, he hit a deer and it bounced right off, the two inch metal pipe mounted on the front had seen to that.

As they rode into town, he thought of Amy and how they'd met. How fast they'd become friends and the nights they would drive out in the country, sit under the stars and just talk. He loved her because she was fun and liked her because she was smart. "Let me ask you something? Brett asked out of the blue. "Do you think Amy really likes my singing or is she just being nice?"

"Dude, you really don't have a clue do you?"

"I just wanted your opinion, that's all."

"They don't make too many like Amy. She's not only smart, she's honest. If she said she likes it, then she likes it."

As the old red truck passed the city limit sign, a young deer dashed across the road. Coming from the opposite direction, a car swerved to miss the deer and veered into the path of Brett's truck. He pulled the wheel and slid sideways onto the shoulder.

As the dust settled, Brett felt something wet on the top of his forehead.

He looked over at Jay.

"You Ok?"

"Dude, that was close."

Brett and Jay jumped out to check on the other driver. He was an older man in his late seventies who really had no business driving but, he was alright. Finally, the shock faded away and after a minute or two they all laughed and drove away.

Pulling up to Amy's house, Brett honked the horn and she came running out with a basket. After practice they usually ate a picnic lunch outside on the lawn. Jay gave Amy a high-five, opened the door and she slid across the seat next to Brett. She gave him a peck on the cheek then saw blood and screamed. "Brett! You're bleeding! What happened?"

"It's nothing. A deer ran across the road and I hit my head."

"About gave me a heart attack." Jay said.

"Really? Are you going to be Ok? Do you need anything? Like maybe …… a blood transfusion?" She asked.

"No, just a little sympathy." Jay said.

Amy and Jay were cousins. It was Jay who introduced Amy to Brett. She and her family had come to Williamsport to visit Jay's family nearly two years before. Jay had invited Brett over for Sunday dinner. Everyone ate while Brett and Amy talked. Brett was not in the least upset that Amy's Dad was moving the family. It was just six months ago that he helped Amy's family move into the big white house on Grant Street. From then on, the two had become inseparable.

Brett drove behind the Chevy dealership and parked next to a Corvette in front of a vacant building. The car belonged to Tom. He was the stereotypical rich kid who amazingly, wasn't spoiled.

Other than the sports car, you'd never known that he had come from a wealthy family. His Dad owned three car dealerships and was making more money than the family could spend. It was Tom's Dad who allowed the band to play in an abandoned warehouse. It was perfect. They could bring the house down and no one cared. The body shop next door made more noise than a freight train.

Brett, Jay and Amy hopped out of the truck, grabbed their gear and walked inside where Luke was already jamming on his favorite guitar. As they settled in for rehearsal, Amy started handing out newly printed sheets of music. Standing in front of the group, Brett wanted to bring them up to date. He had worked hard the past two weeks making calls to different record labels. After more than fifty calls, he finally hit pay dirt. "Now, before we get started,

I want to give you guys an update on promotions." He said.

"Alright. A world tour!" Tom chimed in.

"Well, I talked to Chip from IMS Records and he's agreed to listen to any demos we can put together. The one Amy just put in your hands is called 'Wake Me Up'."

"A song about a hang-over?" Tom asked.

"Not quite. But, I think it'll play."

Jay hit the drums. He was more than ready.

"Let's get started. We're burning daylight."

Wasting no time, the band began to play.

"Pretty fast tempo. On the key of D. Ah one, two, ah one, two, three." Brett said.

As the band began to jam, Amy tried to stuff the leftover lead sheets in Brett's bag and the contents went everywhere. As she madly tried to pick up his things and stuff them back in, she saw the letters. Sitting there staring at them, she counted what seemed to be a dozen unopened letters.

Taking a bite of an apple, she settled against a crate and quickly became lost reading the letters. As Brett sang, he noticed Amy reading something. She was totally absorbed. A moment later he caught her eye and shot her a questioning look. Amy gave him the 'innocent' look and quickly stuffed the letters back. She decided she would ask him about them when they were alone. She could not help but wonder. "Why were these letters never opened? She asked herself.

Just then, the song came to an end.

"Wow! Mega hit." Jay cheered.

"Oh, yea. That'll rock 'em on prom night." Tom said.

Luke pretended to be a fan. Young and female, of course. "Mr. Staggs, can I have your autograph?"

Ignoring him, Brett stopped and looked at Amy. Then, the whole band began to stare. She felt guilty about reading the letters and realized she'd been discovered.

She squirmed while attempting to look innocent.

"What do you think?" Brett asked her.

She tried to act innocent. "About what?"

"The song we just played. What do you think?"

Amy pretended she had heard every word. "Oh, yeah that. Wow it was… I really… liked it. Man, you really nailed that one." No one believed her.

Amy punched the air to show her enthusiasm and smiled suspiciously.

Brett and the band looked at each other, not knowing what to think. Looking back at them, she laughed again nervously. "Ok, keep going".

"Thanks...uh, babe. Alright, this next song is called, 'This Cold Town'."

"Let's do it!" Jay said.

Directing the band, Brett set the rhythm.

"Ok, ready. One, two, ah one, two, three..."

Sitting there, Amy couldn't stop looking at the bag. It didn't make sense. "Why had the letters never been opened?" She thought to herself.

Amy looked up at Brett who wasn't watching. No longer able to resist, she opened the bag and slowly pulled out another letter. Turning it over in her hand, she saw that the paper had turned yellow with age. Careful not to tear the envelope, she took a fingernail file from her purse and opened the seal.

As she continued to read, she again became lost in the words. Brett started the second verse, he looked over at Amy, not believing his eyes.

She was reading the letters!

He didn't know whether to feel embarrassed or angry.

As the song came to an end, Jay made a joke. "I can just hear the girls. Tears in their eyes, Brett, oh, Brett! We love you Brett."

"I'm sure Amy will love that." Brett said.

Brett looked over at her. She was totally lost in one of the letters. She looked as if she was about to cry, totally unaware that the song had ended.

"Amy?"

Unfazed, she turned the page and kept reading.

"Amy!

Surprised, she jumped and realized the whole band was staring at her.

"What?"

"What are you doing?" Brett asked.

"Nothing. I'm just enjoying the music." Amy jumped to her feet and frantically stuffed the letters back in Brett's bag. She was mad at herself. How could she be so careless? She thought.

There were countless questions she was dying to ask, but they would have to wait.

Jay broke the tension by counting the tempo for the next song with his drumsticks. The band broke into the next song and continued to practice.

Amy could hardly concentrate as Brett sang, 'Meet Me at the Restaurant'.

When the practice rehearsal was over, everyone agreed they needed one more session before the Prom.

Outside, everyone loaded their gear.

"Uh, Jay? Amy and I need to run some errands…" Brett said.

"He can ride with me. But, I want to grab a bite first." Tom said.

"I never turn down food. You buyin?" Jay asked.

"Dude, it's my uncle's restaurant."

"Oh, no…, please! Beef on the Hoof. I just hate delicious, corn fed T-bone steak". He paused for a second but, only for the effect. "Ok. But, only if I can wash it down with a cold beer."

Brett shook his head and then looked at Tom.

"Thanks. We'll see you guys later."

Chapter Four

The news about James Dean spread faster than a one armed wallpaper hanger.

From the time Bill and Sanford dropped me off in Salinas, California until I got down to L.A. the next month, that's all I heard was, James Dean this and Jimmy Dean that.

Here was someone who had only made three movies and the last one, Giant, hadn't even been released and everyone acted as if a national hero had died.

Me, I didn't understand the hoopla. I don't mean to sound insensitive. I felt bad for Dean and his family, what family he had.

But, to immortalize the young man I thought was more than he deserved. That's all I'm saying.

Well, after nearly three weeks trying to find a place to explore my music, I finally found a club that wasn't prejudiced to an eastern farm boy musical talent wannabe.

Later on, I met up with a band that needed a lead vocalist and I thought I'd made it to heaven.

We toured for nearly a year and then I thought I had found the woman of my dreams.

Her name was Noreen Baker.

I'd met her at a party after a show and we talked until five the next morning.

Her eyes were as dark as black pearls and her hair too was black as the raven.

She was the most beautiful woman I had ever met and when she smiled, the sun broke from the clouds.

* * * * * *

BRETT AND AMY turned onto Main street and other than the hum of the tires, they rode in silence.

Finally, he couldn't hold it back.

"Why would you go through my letters?" He asked.

"I was putting away your music and they fell out of your bag, Brett! They've never been opened, why?"

"You had no right to go through my stuff!"

"I'm sorry. They just took me by surprise, that's all. I think you would've done the same thing."

"Only if I were a woman."

33

It was too late, the words had already escaped his mouth. He waited for her to strike back.

"You know, I'm going to pretend you didn't say that." Amy said coolly.

Brett knew he had made a cardinal mistake and was ready to take it back. "I'm sorry." He said.

"These letters are a part of your past you haven't told me about. How can we be close if we can't share everything?" She asked.

"I just saw the letters this morning for the first time! Jay was looking through Mom's old trunk and pulled them out. I have no idea where they came from!"

"Your Mom kept them hidden in a trunk?"

"Yea, they've been in there a long time."

"Why would she keep them from you?"

The faded red truck pulled into the parking lot of the baseball field where Brett used to play as a kid.

Getting out of the truck, Brett grabbed his bag. Amy carried the basket lunch.

They walked toward the bleachers and found a spot to sit down and eat.

Amy looked at Brett. "Who is Garrett Arizona?"

"He's my Granddad. Why?"

"He's the one who wrote the letters."

"Are you sure?"

"Well. I only read two or three. There must be at least a dozen."

"Man, this is weird."

"Brett, did you know that your Grandmother died in a car accident?"

"What are you talking about?"

"It's in one of the letters. It had to be written not long after your Dad died. Here, this is the one."

Pulling the letter out of the faded envelope, Amy started to read.

"Dear Brett, I am sorry to hear about your Dad. I can't believe it found him. I tried my best to shield the family from it. Your Grandmother died much the same way. Noreen and I had been together less than a year. We had just moved into a new place. She had fixed it up all nice and pretty.

Then it struck.

I was playing in Sedona when it happened. We had taken a break between sets and one of the local highway patrolman walked in. I could tell from the look on his face something had gone bad.

He told me she'd been killed in an accident. I asked him what kind of accident. He said her car had blown a tire and rolled several times. He felt she died instantly. I don't know why I've never shared it in my letters. I guess maybe to keep you from the pain this thing has caused."

"What is he talking about?" She asked.

"He keeps referring to 'this thing' and 'it'."

"I don't know. My family has never talked about my grandparents." Brett explained.

Amy was surprised at Brett's attitude. He didn't seem to be that interested. She felt she had to investigate this strange behavior further.

"You mean that all these years you've never been curious as to who your grandparents were or what happened to them?"

"We never talked about it."

"Ok, but that shouldn't have kept you.. What I mean is… you don't seem to be the least bit curious. Brett, we're talking about your grandparents, not your next door neighbors!"

"The only time we ever talked about him was when my Dad bought me my first guitar. Dad said that music had been in my family for years and that I might want to take it up. When I showed Mom the guitar and told her what he said, the only thing that came out of her mouth an emphatic, "you just forget about him".

"But, don't you want to find your Grandfather?" Amy probed.

"I'm focused on my career right now, and it's not a part of my plans."

Amy had seen what had really happened.

His Grandfather had actually tried to reach out to him.

"Brett. It's obvious he was trying to reach out to you."

"Look. My Granddad knew all these years where I lived and who I lived with. If he wanted a relationship with me, he could have found a way! But he didn't." Brett said defiantly.

Amy knew it wasn't Brett speaking. It was his mother.

How could she keep him from his Grandfather all those years? What caused her to dislike his Grandfather?" She asked herself. "Maybe hate was a better word." She thought.

Amy felt she just couldn't let it go. Deep down, she just knew Brett would want to find his Grandfather. "Who, in their right mind, wouldn't?" She reasoned to herself.

Looking at him, she couldn't let it go. "Listen, I can't imagine what you are thinking right now. But, your Grandfather must be at least seventy or maybe even eighty. If he's still alive, he's not going to be around forever and if he has passed on, the people who know him won't be around forever, either. So, time is running out here. And, you don't have the rest of your life to think about it. With a little hard work, maybe we can get lucky and find him."

Staring straight ahead, Brett avoided eye contact. He knew what he was about to say was not what she wanted to hear.

"Look, taking the summer off means not starting my job. Besides, it would cause a major argument if I even told my Mom. Just thinking about it gives me a headache."

"I know but, look at it this way, never knowing anything about him will be like a missing piece of life's puzzle. Most people never think about it until it's too late. You may never have this opportunity again." She said.

"Alright," he said. "I'll think about it."

THE NEXT DAY, Brett met the rest of the band for one last rehearsal before prom. It was just a run through before the real thing. Every member took a chorus and gave it all they had. They

38

tried this once in a while to see where it would take them. Brett ran up onto several old crates and jumped down onto the floor. Tom performed a very wild lead guitar solo while jumping around and wound up spinning around on his back. When they were finished, they all felt confident and knew the Prom would be another chance to shine.

Amy and her Mom enjoyed a Vanilla Latte at an outside café as Brett walked over and greeted them.

"Hello, ladies." He said smiling.

"Hi Brett! What happened to your forehead?" Her mother asked

"It's just a scratch. It's nothing really. How was shopping?"

"Shopping? New York has shopping. I feel like I've been to one flea market after another."

Rolling her eyes, Amy leaned over to Brett.

"In case you haven't noticed, Mom is totally spoiled."

Her mother ignored her. "Amy's been telling me about your big plans."

"Yeah, I'm working on a recording contract that could lead to a tour and who knows, maybe a long string of gold records." He said.

"Brett. How old are you?"

"Nineteen."

"Have you ever traveled? I mean, other than Pittsburgh, have you and your family seen what's outside of this small town?"

Allyson Wellock had spent the first forty years of her life living in a cocoon. Married at seventeen, children at twenty, she tolerated her workaholic husband who had little time for travel, and most of all, knowing how to have fun. Amy's mother had made up her mind, long ago, that she would do everything in her power to keep her daughter from making the same mistake and now was her chance.

Brett wasn't sure what Amy's Mom was getting at. "Well, me and my Dad traveled most of Pennsylvania buying horses. But, that's about it." He said.

"Brett, my Grandfather once told me that life is never easy and before I got married, I should have some fun and see the world. He offered me a round trip ticket to New York, but, I just wasn't listening. I had already made up my mind to get married."

Amy's eyes went wide. "Mom, you never told me that." She wasn't used to her mother revealing things to others that she knew nothing about.

"I was waiting to tell Amy about the ticket to Paris I bought her so she could spend two weeks seeing the world and having some fun. I think I'd like to make that… two tickets instead."

"Mother! Are you serious?" Amy screamed.

She looked at her daughter and gave her a smile that said, 'I love you'. Then she said, "Of course I'm serious."

Amy was beside herself as she had always wanted to see Paris. "That's great!"

Brett, was not as excited. "I appreciate the offer, but I'd like to think about it."

"Brett, most of the people in this small town are stuck in a rut. See what this world is all about while you're still young."

"Thanks for the advice." He said.

Looking at her watch, Amy's mother realized what time it was. "You're welcome. Oh, I have an appointment and I'm going to be late. Brett, would you mind dropping Amy off?"

"Sure." Brett said.

"Mom, would you like me to order you something and bring it home?" Amy asked.

"Not at all, honey. You two go enjoy yourselves. I'll grab a bite to eat when I get home."

Picking up her shopping bags, she stopped and turned to Brett. "But, Brett, remember what I said."

"I will."

Brett and Amy ordered sandwiches and talked about the trip to Paris. He had thought about her suggestion to go and find his Grandfather. He knew that now was the time to tell her. "Amy, I thought a lot about what you said and I... What I mean is. Maybe..., you know, later on. Right now, the band needs me. I've got big plans and I'm just not ready to go looking for my Granddad. Besides, I have no idea where he is. I wouldn't even know where to start."

"Fine, but what Mom said makes sense. We have our whole lives ahead of us. The band can wait a few weeks while we find your Grandfather and then we can leave for Paris."

"But, I've spent the last year planning the summer tour. For once, why can't we follow my plan?"

The words came out without thinking. "Well, maybe I'll find someone else who wants to go to Paris."

DRIVING AMY HOME, little conversation took place. She said goodbye, slammed the door and walked inside. Brett laid his forehead on the top of the steering wheel, wondering how the day could have ended this way.

As the old truck pulled into Saddleback Farm, a familiar vehicle was leaving. It was his uncle Marty's.

Marty Staggs was currently a bachelor. He tried marriage, but his wife left after only three months of matrimony.

She said it was his inability to communicate. He reminded her that his asking her time after time to find the TV remote was a form of communication. And, that was the end of their wedded bliss.

Marty fancied himself as the outdoors kind of guy. For him, that meant sitting out on the front porch drinking beer and reading men's magazines. He always wore the same outfit. Flannel shirt, jeans he'd picked up at a Flea Market, a sleeveless hunting jacket, Wolverine Boots and, of course, his Wolverine baseball cap. To Marty, there was no other boot like a Wolverine. Full grain leather, comfort lining, oil, water and slip resistant out-sole. And, a lifetime warranty. His favorite pair had seen better days. Worn-out was more like it. His friends weren't exactly sure whether Marty boasted because of the longevity of his boots or the fact that he was too cheap to buy another pair.

Cigars were his habit. Not the big fat Havanas. He smoked a full bodied cigar made in the Dominican Republic. No one knew who turned him on to those. He never told anyone. Perhaps he thought if too many people bought them, the price would go up.

Marty never really smoked the cigars. He kept the stub in his mouth like an infant with a pacifier.

43

He worked for the Danbury Mill, one of the largest employers in the state. He believed, like most people in Williamsport, 'one employer for life and never retire without a pension'.

Marty was well on his way. He just celebrated fifteen years with Danbury.

Brett pulled alongside Marty's dark blue metallic Chevy pickup and rolled down the window.

Marty was in a hurry. "Hey, Champ! I'm working on getting a table for your Mom. I need you to drop by after school on Wednesday and pick it up."

"Yea, sure." Brett said.

"Say Marty, I want to show you something".

Brett pulled the letters out of his bag. Marty looked like he had seen a ghost. "Where'd you get those?" He asked.

"Up in the attic in Mom's old trunk. Jay found them. It was open."

Marty wasn't in the mood to go into detail. "Listen, your uncle's gonna do you a big favor and not tell your Mom what you have there. And, here's a bit of advice that might save your life. Slowly step away from the truck and put those letters back and forget you ever saw 'em!"

"Why? What's the big deal?" Brett asked.

"Big deal? Did you know your Dad died bringin that old trunk home when your Granddad sent it by freight? Anyone ever tell you that?"

"Yea, I remember. Sort of."

"Listen, I gotta go, I'm late for my poker game. I'll see you on Wednesday."

As Marty peeled out of the driveway, Brett thought he was half crazy, always had been. But, "what did he mean by, might save your life?", He asked himself.

Chapter Five

Standing in the cemetery and looking at her casket, I thought my world had come to an end.

Oh sure, I thought I understood how people felt when they lost someone they cared about but, I had never experienced such pain or loss.

To me, Noreen made me better and always made me feel like I was the most important person in the world.

It took me a long time to get over her. Fact is, I'm not sure I really have. Every time I hear a song that she liked, I think of her.

After nearly two months, I went back to the band. I thought Noreen would want me to move on and so we toured like there was no tomorrow.

I'm not sure how long it was after that, four maybe five years when I was sitting in a café eating breakfast one morning reading about the famous Dean Porsche Spyder.

I guess the fact that I was there the day he died is why I would even be interested.

The article in the paper recounted how many people had died who had anything to do with the James Dean car.

I can't explain it but, that same uneasy feeling came over me. It started the instant Bill, Sanford and I left the crash scene. Something made me feel that someone was looking over my shoulder.

Embarrassed to say that's what I did. I looked over my shoulder and all I saw was a little kid in the next booth staring at me.

For a very long time, that feeling never left.

* * * * * *

THE NEXT DAY AT SCHOOL, Brett looked for Amy. He saw her going into History class as the bell rang. He was too late.

He decided to call her later. Not much to talk about now. He saw the look on her face when he told her that he didn't want to go looking for his Granddad right away.

He always tried to please her, but what she wanted now was asking too much. She just didn't understand.

That night Brett called her. She answered the phone on the fourth ring. Her voice sounded distant.

"Hello."

"Hi, babe."

"Hi." She said in a hollow voice.

"I ordered a special corsage for the Prom. You're still going to the Prom with me, aren't you?"

"Brett, I told you months ago I'd go to the Prom with you. I haven't changed my mind about that, yet."

Relieved, Brett told her he'd see her at school. They said goodbye and hung up.

ON WEDNESDAY, Brett left for school and drove over to Marty's. He promised him he'd pick up the table for his Mom. He found Marty on the porch relaxing in an old rocking chair reading a magazine.

"Hi, Champ. Did you do what I suggested with those letters?" Marty asked.

Brett lied. He wasn't in the mood to argue with anyone, least of all his uncle. "Yea, I put them back and locked the trunk."

"Good. Sit down and rest a spell. Wanna a beer?"

"No thanks, I had some coke on the way over."

"Coke? What kind of coke?"

"The kind you drink out of a bottle."
Brett said.

"Oh, ok. I just thought you meant the
other kind.

Say, your Mom said you start your new
job in two weeks." Marty said.

"Yea. Northwest."

Marty pretended to know the company
intimately. "Very good company."

"It's just a day job. And, it'll pay
the bills while the band gets going."
Brett said.

Other than his nephew, Marty rarely
had anyone to give advice to and he was
not going to pass up this opportunity.

"You know, I'm glad we're havin this
conversation because I'm thinkin you're
about to make the biggest mistake of
your life."

"Marty, I've heard this a million
times. I've made up my mind about the
band. Don't even start."

"I'm not talkin about the band. What
I'm talkin about is your future and you
gettin set for life. Listen Brett, this
area don't have a whole lot of jobs
like the one you just landed. Did you
know that?" Marty asked.

"That's what I've heard." Brett said.

"So, what I'm sayin is, don't bounce
around. Don't jump around. Don't hop

around. Just do your job. Clock in, clock out. But, don't ever, and I mean never lose this job." Marty paused to let his words sink in.

"Understand what I'm sayin? What I'm puttin down? In other words, do you smell what I'm steppin in?" Marty asked with all the wisdom he could muster.

Brett was tired of hearing this same speech. Every time Marty had the chance he just had to brag about his job at Danbury. The many years he had worked there. The number of people he had seniority over. Blah, blah, blah.

"Yea, Yea, same story, different day."

"Good. Just follow my lead and you can retire after twenty-five to thirty years and let Northwest pay you for doin nothin.

You know? One of the old timers at Danbury just retired and he's getting three grand a month to do nothing but sit on his butt!

And, I just passed the fifteen year mark. Fifteen years! Boy does time fly when you're havin fun.

You know what? After fifteen years they can't touch you. That's why they call us the 'Untouchables'."

Brett was tired of hearing this speech and especially this part. "Marty, the only thing you're untouchable with is women. No woman in her right mind would touch you."

"I'm not talkin about women. I'm talkin about your future, boy." Marty said in defense.

"For real, I can show up at work NAKED if I want. Not that I'd ever show up naked, but, they can't touch me and do you wanna know why?"

"Not really." Brett said.

"I have five hundred people under me in seniority. Five hundred!"

"Surely you're not gonna talk about the benefits!" Brett resigned.

Marty's face lit up. He had forgotten about the benefits at Danbury.

"Oh, yea! The beney's". He said.

Brett realized his mistake. "Here we go!"

"I have four weeks of vacation and TEN sick days. Even better, they PAY me to see a Chiro-Practor. And, you know what? She's good lookin and her adjustments, they're more like a massage.

And, get this! My funeral plan is part of my pension plan! And it's ALL paid for! Ha, Ha, Ha. I mean, I am set! And, so can you Brett, if you don't blow it. Stay with Northwest and put in your twenty-five to thirty years and RETIRE. Then, they have to pay while you sit on your keyster.

Understand what I'm saying?"

"Wow, Marty, you've introduced a whole new paradigm." Brett said.

"Uh, yea, sure. Paradigm. Pair a nickels. Two cents to rub together. That there is knowledge you can take with you."

Having no children of his own, Marty was proud of himself for sharing such rare words of insight and wisdom with his nephew. With no father, he felt it was the least he could do for the poor boy.

"Now, you can thank me for the advice by helpin me load your Mom's new table onto your truck."

Stepping off the porch, Brett and Marty struggled to get the solid oak table onto Brett's pickup. It was heavy. Resting against the old truck, Brett noticed Marty was staring at his shoes.

"What are you looking at?"

"You still wearing moccasins?"

"They're not moccasins." Brett insisted.

"You can't wear those to work, you know." Marty said.

"Why not? They're comfortable."

"OSHA."

"What's that?"

"Occupational…..Safety….Hazard, Uh……..
California, somethin or another. It's a
safety law and it says you have to wear
boots.

Now, what I recommend are Wolverines.
The toughest, longest lasting, sexist
boot ever made. You see, when I first
started workin, more'n fifteen years
ago…"

Brett listened for a few minutes and
finally told Marty he had to go.

THAT AFTERNOON, Brett drove up to
Lookout Point. The mountain was part of
the Ridge and Valley section west of
the Appalachian Mountains. It was here
that he used to spend weekends with his
Dad fishing. Of all the places on
earth, it was a quiet and peaceful
place where he could see for miles and
contemplate the future. Here is where
the earth met the sky and every problem
seemed small next to the higher order
of the universe. He thought about the
last few days and the conversations
he'd heard that had been weighing on
his mind. The first conversation had
started when he had first applied for a
job at Northwest.

"So, how long were you with Danbury
before you got laid off?" The stranger
had said.

"Thirteen years." The other worker   ·
replied.

"That's too bad. I hear Northwest has the best benefit and pension plan anywhere."

"Yea, that's what I heard. I just want to find a place where I can hang my hat for another ten and retire."

"Amen to that."

"I heard Northwest got that bid for government freight. That means, for the next two years, people will be working six to seven days a week, twelve hours a day."

"I don't mind the hours. Me and the old lady are separated and I like all the overtime I can get."

The other conversation he overheard was at the Midtown diner while he was grabbing a bite to eat. As usual, the place was packed. He had been sitting at the far side of the counter eating a burger when he overheard an older couple in the next booth.

"Maybelle said that Tom and Caroline are moving to Pittsburgh to start their own business." The woman gossiped.

"Starting your own business is risky." Her husband of thirty years replied.

"She said Tom couldn't see clocking in everyday for doing the same job."

"Why can't he just get a real job that offers health insurance, retirement and a pension?"

"That's what a man with a family should do. Get a real job that offers security."

"I can't understand why they wouldn't want a regular paycheck."

"That's what I'm saying. I don't particularly like my job. It's not fun. The fun should start when someone retires."

As Brett stared into the mist that covered the mountain in the distance, he thought about his conversation with Marty and the people he'd overheard. He realized he was at a pivotal moment in his life and thought about what he really wanted. Glad he had taken the time to think, a new plan began to form in his mind. He realized it wasn't what he wanted to do but, it was exactly what he had to do.

ON SATURDAY, over five hundred people packed the huge gymnasium that had been transformed into another world of dark colored curtains, huge arrangements of decorative foliage and twenty foot portable statues of celebrities.

The crowd milled around the floor waiting for the music to start.

Backstage, Brett and the band were getting their instruments ready.

Jay felt a little nauseous.

"I think I'm going to throw up." He said.

Brett tried to calm his nerves.

"You'll be fine. Just keep taking deep breaths."

Back in the gymnasium, the Emcee took the stage. "Ok, everyone. Welcome to the Fifty-Sixth Annual High School Prom! We have a real treat for you tonight. Give it up for The Long Time Darlings!"

The band ran on stage and the crowd offered a loud applause along with cat calls. Next, someone yelled from the back.

"Jay, I love you!"

The band opened with the song called, 'This Cold Town'. As Brett and the band played, everyone was dancing and having a great time. Amy sat next to her best friend Janine whose date had the flu and couldn't make it. Amy was glad to have a friend to hang out with. When Brett played a gig it wasn't like being on a date, it was like being at a dance all alone. As they enjoyed the music, the two girls began to talk.

Janine felt Amy's sadness.

"So, how's it going with Brett?"

"Alright, I guess." Amy said.

She tried to cheer her up. "Just, alright? He's so hot! Most girls would kill to be going out with him."

"He is the closest thing to a rock star in this town, but I'm finding it's not that easy."

"Like what?"

"Like his Mom. Like his plans. He's very ridged about the way he wants things to go. It always has to be his way or no way. And, sometimes it feels like there's no room for what I want."

As 'This Cold Town' came to a close, Janine took Amy's hand in hers and looked into her eyes.

"Like, Amy, I had no idea. It'll be okay. Come on, let's dance."

The two girls jumped to their feet and moved toward the stage. Amy hadn't heard this song before and instead of dancing she and Janine stood and watched the band play. The rest of the crowd gathered around the stage and listened. As the song played, Amy was torn. She loved the sound of his voice and the way he sang to her. She thought about him writing a new song especially for her, this song. But, they were so different. They were opposites in many ways. As Brett sang, Amy wondered how they could ever reconcile it all. Thinking to herself, she decided that she must tell him.

As the song ended, the crowd gave a big round of applause.

Brett stepped to the microphone. "This next song I want to dedicate to my girlfriend, Amy."

Brett pointed toward Amy and the crowd turned to look at her. Embarrassed, she waved back as the band began to play the last song called, 'The Puzzle'. As the band played, Amy fought back tears. She moved toward the back of the gymnasium. Janine followed her. Overcome with emotion, Amy walked outside and the two girls stood under a tree.

"Amy, what is it?"

"I just can't do it. I can't stay with Brett. It's not going to work."

"What are you talking about? Everyone goes through this. It's never perfect."

"No, Janine. You don't understand. I can't go through life like this!"

"Like what?"

"Like waiting in the wings while he fulfills all of his plans. That's not going to happen."

Janine followed as Amy walked back to the Prom with purpose. She knew she had to tell him tonight. Janine tried to keep up with her.

"Amy, wait a minute!"

As the Prom ended, Brett found Amy coming out of the ladies room. They both had something they needed to say and walked to his truck. Shrouded in a thick silence, they drove away without saying a word. Fifteen minutes later, they arrived at Riverfront Gardens, a twenty acre park of beautiful trees that followed the Susquehanna River that flowed through the hills and valleys of central Pennsylvania.

Fifty yards upstream, the final night time Riverboat Tour docked and slowly but surely, twenty enthusiastic people walked down the wooden plank onto solid ground. The night was full of life as they found a park bench and sat down.

Brett couldn't wait to tell her. "Amy, there's something I want to say to you…"

"No, wait. There's something I have to say first." She said.

"I Am Here For You was beautiful. I loved the way you sang it to me."

She paused and then took a deep breath.

"You really have a gift."

"That was for you." He said.

"I know and… 'The Puzzle', I assume you had your Grandfather's letters in mind when you wrote it?" She asked.

"Yes. The letters, everything, it's all a puzzle and I need your help." Brett said.

"But, this is something you should …"

"Wait, just hear me out!"

"Fine, go ahead." She said.

"I've been thinking about a lot of things lately.

And, I've changed my mind… I don't want to start a new job, I want to…"

"But, you said you wanted that job. You worked hard to find it, remember?"

"I know, but that's not who I am!"

"Then, WHO are you, Brett Staggs? Because, honestly, that I can't figure out!"

"Look! For a long time, I've been listening to people tell me what my life should be. And, it's not who I am and it's not what I want."

"Then, what do you want?" She demanded.

Brett turned and looked into her eyes. "I want you." He said softly.

His words had broken her facade. He was no longer a stranger to her.

Holding back tears, she wanted to know more. "You do?"

"Yes." He said. "And, I want to make music, not punch a clock for thirty years."

"Who said you had to punch a clock?" She wondered out loud.

"Marty. What a moron." Brett said.

"Marty?" Amy asked in confusion.

"It's a long story."

"What about your Grandfather?"

"I've changed my mind. I've read every letter twice and now I understand what he was trying to do. He wanted to reach out to me even though Mom did everything she could to stop him. I don't think I could live with myself if he died without ever meeting him."

Brett knew that he probably couldn't find his Grandfather without her and if she were to help him now, he would have to show her that he could be humble.

"And, you're good at this type of thing. You're actually…. smarter… than I am, and I'm asking you to help me before it's too late."

His words surprised her. "What did you say?"

"Which part?" He asked.

"The last part." She said.

"I don't think I could live with myself if I didn't find him?"

"No, I mean the part right after that. Something about.. SMART." She reminded him.

For a second, Brett was confused and wasn't sure what she was getting at. But then, he finally got it.

"What? Oh… ok, alright, I admit it. You're smarter than I am."

Putting his arm around her, he did his best to win her over.

"Amy, listen. If you help me, I think we can find him."

"You should find him but, I want to go to Paris this summer. How does that fit into your plans?"

Knowing her, he was prepared and ready for this particular question. "I was getting to that. First we can find my Granddad, then we can go to Paris and then we can take it one day at a time."

"Can you say that last part again? I like hearing it."

"Which part?" He asked jokingly.

Looking into each other's eyes, they embraced. He brought his lips to hers and they kissed as if it were the very first time.

Amy agreed to help Brett find his Grandfather and they decided to leave the day after graduation.

They knew it would not be easy but, somehow they would find him.

THE NEXT TWO WEEKS flew by. On the evening right before their scheduled departure, Brett was in the attic packing when he heard his favorite ring tone.

It was Amy.

"Brett, have you told your Mom, yet?" She asked.

"What's the hurry?" He said without thinking.

She couldn't believe what she had just heard. "What's the hurry?" She asked. "We're leaving in the morning and you can't just go without telling her."

"I know."

"I am not going to spend the rest of my life with a procrastinator. We've talked about it for two weeks. You have to tell your Mom what you've decided to do."

"Alright. I'll tell her tonight." He assured her.

"Ok, but when you pick me up in the morning, my bags will be packed.

But, if I see any deceit in your eyes that says you haven't told her. I'm not going."

"Alright for god's sake, I'll tell her."

Looking at his watch, Brett realized how late it was and in thirty minutes, his Mom would be fast asleep. If he was going to tell her, it would have to be now or never.

Walking into the kitchen, Brett found his Mom baking his favorite cookies. Why he thought, at this very moment, did she have to be doing something nice for him when he knew what he had to say.

"Hey honey! I'm making you some cookies for tomorrow. They'll be ready in just a minute."

"Thanks Mom. But, there's something I need to talk to you about."

"Is it Amy? Is everything OK?" Sue inquired.

"We're fine. It's something else. Listen…."

Brett paused as he tried to find the courage to tell her.

"I found the letters in the attic. The trunk was open and I found them. I read every one of them!"

Surprised, Sue put her hand over her chest. "You did what?"

"I read the letters from Granddad!"

"Jonathan Brett Staggs. Who the hell do you think you are? What gives you the right to go through my trunk?"

"Mom, the letters were addressed to me! You hid them all these years."

"Brett, please don't ever touch that trunk again! Do you hear me? You have no idea what you're dealing with."

"Yes I do! He's my Granddad and he tried to reach out to me and you stopped him!"

"Yes I stopped him. And, for good reason!"

"What could possibly give you the right to keep me from knowing who my Granddad was?"

Sue didn't respond. She looked out the window at the faded red truck parked in the driveway. If he had his way, she knew it would soon take him away from her.

Putting both hands on the kitchen counter, somehow, she regained her composure. "Brett... Honey... I never really knew him.

Uncle Jim and Irene didn't tell me about your Granddad until I was older. All that time, I thought they were my parents.

After your Dad and I were married, I tried to forget him.

Then you were born and that's when the letters started to come.

I thought about meeting him and then it started to happen."

"What started to happen?" Brett asked.

"People talk, Brett. Marty told your Dad what they were saying. We heard some terrible things that involved your Granddad."

"Like, what?"

"I'd rather not discuss it."

"Mom, basing your entire life on nothing but suspicion and rumor is ... is just stupid!"

"You little bastard! Don't be so naïve. Let me spell it out for you.

Your Granddad's bride was killed in a car wreck less than a year after they were married!

Then we heard someone who played in a band with him in Pittsburgh was killed, driving his truck.

I could go on. But, I think that your own father's death in a car wreck bringing that trunk home would be enough even for you!"

Immediately, Sue stormed out of the kitchen and slammed her bedroom door.

Standing there alone, all Brett could hear was the kitchen clock on the wall.

It was almost eleven o'clock.

Stepping in front of his bathroom mirror he stared back at himself. He looked exhausted and felt it down to his bones.

The last few weeks had been intense with finals and band rehearsals. On top of it all, he hadn't been sleeping well. He laid in bed half the night thinking about the trip and where it might take them. Something in the pit of his stomach told him that this journey wasn't going to be easy.

Maybe his mother was right. Maybe he should forget it, but the plan was set and he and Amy were itching for a new adventure. Anything away from this town and all the frustrations it had brought him.

He hoped that someday his Mother would forgive him. If she knew they were leaving in the morning she wouldn't be thinking about sleep, pills or no pills.

As he looked out the window, Brett saw the Moon rising above the horizon in the east. He knew that by this time her medication had kicked in and that he could begin the first stage of their plan. Quietly, he loaded his luggage in the back of the truck. He had parked at the top of the hill headed down the drive.

In the morning, all he had to do was to sneak down stairs, get in the truck and coast out the front gate. It was down- hill from there.

A few hundred yards down the road, he would pop the clutch and be on his way. Brett decided to sleep in the attic. He didn't want to wake her on the way out in the morning.

Chapter Six

After the funeral, I drove straight to Pennsylvania. My little sweetheart slept most of the way.

Having someone else raise our little baby girl was the hardest thing I've ever had to do.

Funny thing, most of the band wanted me to keep her. I know they had good intentions, I suppose. Little Sue reminded them of home and when you're on the road, having a little bit of home with you isn't all bad.

They had become fond of her but, I knew what I had to do. It was the only thing I could do. I mean, how could a musician take care of a newborn and be on the road at the same time?

What kind of life would a child have with no Mom and her Dad is constantly on some kind of tour? Playing all night until the sun comes up.

That's the point I'm trying to make.

So, I took little Sue to my Brother and Sister-in-law and they were happy to take her in.

It was two in the morning when I got there. I hated to wake them up.

But, I'll never forget the look on Irene's face when I handed our little

*baby girl to her. She had the same look
Noreen had when she held her.*

It was sheer happiness.

*I'm not sure what sort of father I
would have been. I guess I never will
know. It doesn't matter now.*

*Looking back, I don't think I would
want any kids around, considering what
I've been through.*

* * * * * *

AT SIX O'CLOCK, Brett's alarm on his
cell phone went off. Standing to
stretch, he couldn't believe it was
already morning. It felt like he had
only been asleep for five minutes.

Slowly, he descended the wooden
staircase to the attic. The boards
squeaked louder than he could remember.

Walking to the truck and opening the
door, Brett threw his back-pack on the
front seat. He hated the fact that he
couldn't have a cup of coffee to start
the morning but, caffeine would have to
wait. He couldn't risk waking his Mom.

Coasting down the drive and almost to
the bottom of the hill, Brett popped
the clutch and began to climb onto the
main road when out of nowhere another
truck pulled across and blocked his

path. Slamming on the brakes, Brett jumped out of the truck.

He was furious.

"What the hell are you doing?"

"Mornin Champ!"

"You're in my way. I've made up my mind and you can't stop me!"

"Stop you? Shoot, I'm goin with you!"

"What?"

"I said. I'm goin with you."

"No, Marty, you are not going with me!"

"Why, not?"

"Because I said so, that's why."

"Brett, I can help you." Marty explained.

"How did you know I was leaving?" Brett asked.

"Your Mom called me late last night. You've got her real worried and she told me what you had in mind. You see, the way I figured it, if it were me I'd sneak out in the cover of darkness. You know, before the Roosters were up, when it's all quiet and nobody's up and around, you know, like about now.

And, sure enough, here you are!"

"Marty, this is not part of my plan. Get out of my way! I've got to go! Amy's waiting and Mom will be up soon."

"How about this?" Marty compromised. "Let me ride on into town and if I can't convince you to take me with you then you can go on without me, fair enough?"

Brett looked back at the still dark house. Slapping his hand against the truck, he realized he had no choice, he had to leave now.

"Alright, get in. You can ride with me to Amy's but, that's as far as you go."

Marty pulled onto the shoulder and realized he'd have to call Sue later. She would wonder why his truck was parked out front.

Closing the door, Brett hit the accelerator, angry that the trip was not starting out as he had planned.

"Don't even think for a second you're going to talk me into letting you go."

"Why not? I know I can help you." Marty said.

"Marty, I don't need your help."

"Yes you do."

"How could you possibly think about going? You just told me the other day you've used up all your vacation time."

"No, unfortunately, there won't be any more vacations. I got the pink slip yesterday. At this very moment, I am unemployed."

"What?"

"Yessir, the unthinkable has just happened. Yours truly is out of a freakin job. They laid off the entire department yesterday. I can't believe it. They let go more than a hundred people!" Marty said.

"What happened to the 'Untouchables'?"

"What?"

"The 'Untouchables', remember?" Brett reminded him. "You said you could go to work NAKED and they couldn't touch you. What happened to that?"

"Well..."

"What happened to...

Brett, don't bounce around.

Brett, don't hop around.

Brett, just do your job. You know, clock in, clock out. Remember?

Stay with Northwest, you can retire after 30 years! What happened to all that?" Brett demanded.

Marty was taken aback. He had never heard Brett string this many words together at one time.

72

"Why are you so uptight? I'm the one who's been laid off here and I'm not cryin over my beer. Which reminds me, did you bring any?"

"Any what?"

"Beer! You can't plan a road trip without beer."

"Marty! Stop trying to distract me from the subject. You're not going!"

"Brett. I'm telling you. I can help you. If you'd just hear me out."

Brett's truck pulled into the driveway as Amy came out the front door with her luggage. Surprised, her eyes went wide as she looked at him.

"Marty, what are you doing here?" She asked.

Marty avoided the question. He knew Brett would explain it for him. "Mornin, Amy! Did you pack any beer?"

Brett looked at Amy and took her luggage and put it behind the front passenger seat.

"He's trying to convince me that we should take him with us."

Marty interrupted. "I've been tryin to explain, I'm the one that can help put all the pieces together."

"How can you not understand the words- You're not going!" Brett said emphatically.

"Brett. You've never met your Granddad. I have. You've don't know what he looks like, I do."

Brett had never in his life heard this before.

"You met my Granddad?" Brett asked."

"Yea, that's what I've been tryin to tell you."

Brett wasn't convinced. "Ok, where did you meet him?"

"Well, after I started at the mill, they transferred me to Pittsburgh in '86. I was only there for a couple a years and then I came back. After work, me and a few of the boys would go to the Old Mill Tavern in Polish Hill for a beer and your Granddad used to play there.

He was one helluva guitar player." Marty said.

For a moment, Brett thought about it. If what Marty said was true, maybe he could help find his Granddad.

"So… you really think we can find him?" Brett asked.

"Unless, he's already dead and walked through the Pearly Gates, yea, I think we can find him."

Amy rolled her eyes. She had been looking forward to this trip for two weeks and had hardly slept at all.

"Brett, can I speak to you for a minute?" She asked.

"Sure, babe."

Amy was visibly upset as they stepped onto the porch. She thought this would be their trip, a chance to spend some time alone, but that idea was fading fast.

"I thought this was going to be our trip. Taking him with us changes everything."

"Look. I don't want him to go either, but if he can help us..."

She cut him off.

"Look at him! I'm looking at a goat herder. He's all scruffy and he smells."

Brett turned and looked him up and down. Marty didn't notice. He was too busy cutting his finger nails with his pocket knife. "Yea, I see what you mean."

"Why can't it be just the two of us?" She asked

"I understand. But look, I think he can help us, at least in Pittsburgh..."

Brett stopped. He had an idea that just might work. "Hey, that's it! We can take him to Pittsburgh. Find out what we can there, and I'll buy him a bus ticket and send him back. That way, he'll only be with us for a day, maybe two at the most. You can put up with him for a day or two can't you?"

Amy had her arms crossed and was looking down, she was obviously disappointed. The old truck didn't have a lot of extra room even though it was the extended cab version. But, she thought that if Marty could help, even for just a day or two, she could handle it. But, definitely not more than a couple of days, she thought.

"Ok, but, only for a day or two or I'll be the one on that bus instead of him."

"Alright, let's get going." Brett said.

SQUEEZING INTO THE CAB of the old truck, they turned onto Interstate 180. Twenty minutes later, Brett pulled into a Pancake House and grabbed his backpack and a map.

Sitting in a corner booth, a Waitress was writing everyone's order. She looked like she had been up all night and she had.

"So, I have two orders of Bacon & Eggs. One scrambled and the other over easy. One with whole wheat toast and the other with pancakes. One order of biscuits and gravy.

Can I get you anything else?" She asked.

Marty didn't look up as he spoke to the Waitress.

"I'd like some ketchup for my eggs."

"Sure, honey." The Waitress took their menus and was off to the kitchen.

As Amy stared at Marty, Brett decided to take the letters out of his back-pack and opened up a map.

"Marty, how rude! The Waitress asked you nicely if you'd like anything else.

Haven't you ever heard of the word, Please?" She said.

"Oh sure. When I was stopped for speeding last week, I told the officer, Please don't give me a ticket. Didn't work. He gave me one anyway."

"Marty, if you ever want to get ahead in life, you have to be polite."

"Ok, I'm sorry I offended you. I'll insert that word into my vocabulary."

Pretending he hadn't heard their bickering, Brett looked up from the map.

"Alright, I've read every letter twice and it's obvious where we should start. I've got it all planned out."

"Where's that?" Marty asked.

"Pittsburgh. Of all the addresses on the letters, it's the closest."

"It's also the place where he first started writing from." Amy said.

Marty was not sure Pittsburgh was the right place to start. He knew there were letters from different places and the clock was ticking.

"But, if he started writin from Pittsburgh in '86, that's nearly twenty years ago. I'm tellin you, there's nothing in Pittsburgh. I should know. It'll waste a whole lot of time and time is what we don't have. Don't you think we should start with the last letter and head straight there?" Marty asked.

Amy gave Brett a look. She wasn't sure how to answer him.

"Brett, where did he write the last letter from?" She asked.

"Memphis." He answered.

That was music to Marty's ears.

"There you go! Memphis. Elvis Presley! He probably played with Elvis before he died." Marty said.

Brett started to laugh. "Marty! Elvis Presley died in 1977. My Granddad wrote his last letter from Memphis.. let's see... in 2000.

There's no way he played with Elvis!"

"Marty. Pittsburgh is close." Amy said. "And, it's a starting point. Who knows, we may learn something we can use later."

"Ok. But, I'm tellin you. We won't find anything in Pittsburgh." Marty said.

It was a close call as Amy breathed a sigh of relief. She could not see traveling with Marty more than a few days.

"Marty, how old do you think he is?" Brett asked.

Distracted, Marty looked out the window as two women were getting out of a new sports car. Watching women was his favorite past time. "Who, your Granddad?" He said finally.

"No, Michael Jackson." Brett said.

"Sorry, the caffeine hasn't kicked in. Let's see. When I saw him in the eighties, he looked late forties, early fifties."

"That's about right. He said he left California when he was twenty." Brett said.

"What year was your Mom born?" Amy asked.

"1957." Brett said.

Amy tried to put the pieces together. "Well, if he was in his twenties when she was born, that would mean he was born sometime in the 1930's. That means he's in his seventies and could still be around."

"What's the date on the postmark from Pittsburgh?" Marty asked.

"July of '86. Why?" Amy asked.

"I'm getting all confused with these dates." Marty said.

"Here, let me write all this down. We need a timeline." Amy grabbed a pen and started writing. "Ok. So, he moved from somewhere in California to Pittsburgh in '86 and starts writing letters.

Brett, what year did your Dad pass?" Amy asked.

"In 2000."

Marty was confused. "What does that have to do with anything?"

"2000 was the year of his last letter." Brett answered.

"He sent it from Memphis." Amy said.

"Undoubtedly, Mom wasn't responding to his letters. He must have heard about Dad's accident and stopped writing." Brett explained.

"That makes sense." Amy said.

"You know, I haven't even looked at those letters since your Mom showed them to me. How many places did he write from?" Marty wondered.

Amy took out the letters and started to lay them out on the table. "Let's see. Let me arrange them. We know about Pittsburgh and Memphis. And, after Pittsburgh he wrote from Charleston, West Virginia, in '87." Amy revealed.

"Why would he leave Pittsburgh so soon? He wasn't there very long." Brett asked.

"He wasn't in any of these places very long." Amy said.

"How many places did he write from?" Marty asked.

Amy started counting the letters.

"Let's see, wow! Thirteen places in fifteen years!" She said.

Marty laughed out loud. "The good old baker's dozen, lucky thirteen!"

Just then, the Waitress appeared with their food. "Here's your order. Eggs, biscuits and gravy. Anything else?" She asked.

"Uh, yea. Could I get some ketchup, please?" Asked Marty.

The Waitress sensed a more pleasant customer and smiled at Marty. "Sure thing. I'll be right back."

"Very good Marty! See, that wasn't so hard." Amy said.

"No, that wasn't so hard. Divorce court? Now, that was hard." Marty said.

While eating, they discussed how many places they would have to visit. The task of finding Garrett Arizona seemed daunting. Brett looked at the map one more time.

"Amy, what was the return address in Pittsburgh?"

"It was 1201 E. Main, Apt 12, Pittsburgh."

"Marty, where did you say you met my Granddad?" Brett asked.

"The Old Mill Tavern. Down on Penn Ave." He said.

Brett felt good about their plan and the fact that they had more than one place to check. "Well, at least we have two places to start looking."

As they drove east, Marty was ready to hear some music and handed Brett a CD of his favorite artist.

"Marty, I'm not playing your 'He stole my wife - She cheated on me, Country Music'." Brett said.

"Come one, Brett. I can't stand your drum bangin. Let's alternate. I'll go crazy if we don't." Marty replied.

"You're already past crazy." Brett laughed.

Marty decided to negotiate. "Just play one song of mine and one of yours. Then it'll be fair."

"Brett, let Marty hear one song." Amy said.

"Alright, but I warned you."

"Amy, can you roll up your window? I can't hear the music. It's too noisy back here."

"No, Marty. I won't roll up the window. You smell bad and I'd faint if I had to roll it up.

When was the last time you took a bath?" She asked.

"Tuesday. I never miss taking a bath on Tuesday." Marty said.

"It's Sunday! That's almost a week ago?"

"So, what's wrong with that?"

Putting a CD of Marty's into the audio player, Brett tried to tolerate his music, unsuccessfully. "Marty, your music is terrible. You really listen to that?" He asked.

"All day long man." Marty said smiling.

"Ok, but only one song. I can't stand it." Brett said.

THE OLD RED TRUCK and its music barreled down the Interstate. After several stops, the three made it to

Pittsburgh and pulled into the Holliday Motel. Walking inside, the three stopped at the front desk. The place seemed deserted.

"Does anyone work here? Where's the help?" Brett asked.

"Watching old reruns, I'm sure." Marty said.

Just then, a woman came up to the counter.

"Hi, can I help you?" She asked.

"Yes, we'd like a room with two beds and a roll away." Brett said.

"Surely. How many in your party?"

"Three." Brett said.

"Ok, sir. You'll be in room 312. How many keys?" The desk clerk asked.

"Three, please."

"Ok, here you go. Take the elevator on your right to the third floor."

"Thanks." Brett picked up the keys. "Say, what's the easiest way to get to Main Street from here?" He asked.

"Oh, that's easy, Sir. Just go right out of the parking lot three blocks and turn right onto Third Street and follow it about a mile to Main.

It's not hard to find." She said.

When they finally made it to the room, Brett opened the curtains to let the light in. Pulling them back, the window revealed a perfect view of downtown Pittsburgh.

They had lots of questions that needed to be answered and they hoped this town would tell them something.

AFTER AN HOUR, they climbed back into the pickup and turned onto Main Street. Riding several blocks, they stopped in front of an apartment building that had seen better days.

Amy took out her notepad as they stood in front of the Manager's office while Brett knocked several times.

The front door was hidden by a rusty screen door. After several tries, no one answered.

Standing in front of the screen door, Amy practically yelled. "Hello, is anyone here?"

"This place has a unique fragrance." Marty said.

"No Marty, you're smelling yourself for the very first time." Amy said.

"Now, who's being offensive?" He asked.

"Your lack of personal hygiene is offensive, and if…" Amy started.

"That's enough, you guys. Can't we stay focused for a few minutes?" Brett asked.

Finally, an older woman came to the door. It was obvious she had been sleeping as her hair was standing straight up. She was less concerned about her looks than the three peering through the door. Standing perfectly still, she looked the three up and down. "Yes, can I help you?" She asked.

"We're looking for the Manager." Brett said.

"I'm the Manager. Are you needing an apartment?" She asked.

"No, not exactly."

"Are you from the immigration office?" The Manager worried.

"No. Nothing like that." Brett reassured her.

Relieved, she opened the door and stepped out. "Oh, alright. What can I do for you?" She asked.

"My Granddad used to live here and we're looking for him." Brett said.

"What's his name?"

"Garrett Arizona."

"I don't recall anyone by that name. Are you sure he lived here?" She asked.

"Yes. We're very sure. He lived in apartment twelve. We have a letter with this return address on it." Amy said.

Amy showed the woman the aged letter. She looked at it and feeling more at ease, she invited them in.

Sifting through her records, she found a three by five card with more information. The card explained everything. "I'm sorry I can't help you. My late husband and I bought this property in '87 when he retired. I never met your Grandfather. All I can tell you is that apartment twelve had already been remodeled when we took over. The previous owners said there was a mysterious fire that broke out. They included it in their disclosure. Didn't want to get sued and all that. Just so happens, an old bachelor moved in and lived there until he died last week. We're cleaning it now." She explained.

"Could we see it?" Amy asked.

"Oh, sure. But, it's a mess. We're painting and replacing the carpet." She said.

"We would still like to see it." Brett confirmed.

"Well, come on then. Let me get my keys."

The four made their way to the apartment. It was a quiet place with a small courtyard, picnic table and chairs. The door was open when they got there. The painters were rolling fresh paint on the living room walls. The apartment was very small with one bedroom, a bath and a small kitchen. After looking inside for a few minutes, the woman led them into the living room.

"Well here it is. I'm sorry I couldn't help you anymore." She said.

"We appreciate your help." Amy said.

"Where are you staying?" She asked.

"At the Holliday Motel." Brett said.

"I sure wish you all luck."

"Thank you." Amy said.

PULLING UP TO THE Old Mill Tavern, Amy and Brett were hopeful they would learn something that would lead them to his Grandfather. Marty shook his head.

"I'm telling you this place is a waste of time. He hasn't lived here in nearly twenty years. A lot can change in that amount of time. The woman didn't even know him. And, I'm sure this place will be the same." Marty said.

"Oh yea, we had someone here in '86 by that name, but he's long gone. Ok, thank you." Marty said mockingly. "We already knew that! We're wasting time, Brett. Your Granddad could be on his deathbed right now and we're stuck in Pittsburgh."

"Marty, we have to start somewhere and this is the logical place." Amy said.

"I'm just saying, we're not going to learn anything until we get closer to his last letter." Marty said.

"Look, we don't have to be here long. We find out what we can and then we'll know for sure." Brett said.

"One thing we will find out." Marty said.

"What's that?" Amy asked.

"What brand of beer he drank."

"You are such an alcoholic."

Walking into the Old Mill Tavern, They found the place practically empty. A woman behind the bar served a beer to an older man who took a long slow pull.

"Nope, he's not here. Let's go." Marty joked.

"Relax, Marty. Let's follow our plan. I'll buy you a beer and let's see what we can find out." Brett said.

"This plan of yours is getting us nowhere." Marty replied.

They found a table near the bar and the lady bartender walked over. "Hi folks. What'll it be?" She asked.

"I'll have a coke." Brett said.

"Me too." Amy said.

"I'll have an Iron City on Tap, sweetheart." Marty said.

As she walked away with their order, Marty slowly turned and looked around the room.

"Man, this place has changed." He said.

Brett looked around, trying to imagine what it was like sitting and listening to his Granddad play his music. "So, where did you meet my Granddad?" Brett asked.

"They had a small stage and a dance floor over there in the corner." Marty said.

On the nights your Granddad played, the place was packed. He really could bring in a crowd.

"So, how did you meet him?"

"Meet him? I said I saw him."

"Marty, I specifically remember you saying, you met him." Brett said.

"Met him, saw him. I told you I knew what he looked like and you didn't. That was the point I was trying to make." Marty said.

"Oh good. Drinks." Amy said.

"Here you are. Anything else?"

"The place has changed a lot since '86." Marty said.

"Oh yea, the Tavern's been in the same family for three generations. The grandson completely remodeled it last year." The Bartender said.

"My name is Marty and this is Brett and Amy."

"Nice to meet you."

"Brett here, is trying to locate his Grandfather, Garrett Arizona. I saw him play here in '86." Marty said.

"You should talk to Leonard. He's the second generation. He's retired but, he still comes in everyday. I'll tell him to come over when he gets here."

"Thank you." Marty said.

"Not bad. When you want to, you can be polite." Amy said.

"Actually, I just have a way with women."

"Then why have you been single all these years?" She asked.

"How many hens do you count in the henhouse and how many Roosters? There you go, at least ten to one.

I've been tied down to one woman and it's not for me. I like havin my pick of the henhouse." Marty said.

"Marty, I don't know what henhouse you're talking about, but the hens must have no sense of smell." Amy said.

"Very funny. Haven't you heard of Pheromones?" He asked.

"Yes, but what does that have to do with chickens?" Amy asked.

"I'm talking about smell. I have a higher level of Pheromones than most men. That's why I attract women so easily." Marty explained.

"The only thing that you attract, are flies." Amy said.

"You know, I understand your age has not permitted you to amass a great deal of knowledge on the subject and that's the reason I am not offended by your sense of humor and..."

Brett interrupted. "Marty, see that old guy that just came in. Could that be Leonard?"

"He's a lot older but yea, I think that's him." Marty said.

Leonard Matthews had never known any other profession than the bar business. His father had started the Tavern in 1938. He was a jolly fellow who had never met a stranger. Bald, but handsome, Leonard was retired but never missed a day coming into the bar, unless of course, he was on vacation with his wife, Gladys. She loved the sun and the beaches of Mexico. He, on the other hand, loved people. Especially, those who dared to follow their dreams. The community of performers in Pittsburgh revered Leonard because he had a soft heart for musicians and supported them breaking into the business. The lady bartender spoke to Leonard and pointed toward them. Leonard smiled and headed over to the table. They could see by his friendly manner why the Tavern was still in business.

"Well hello." He said with a grin that said they were always welcome in his establishment. "I'm Leonard. Katie said you were looking for someone. Mind if I sit down? The old legs aren't what they used to be."

"Sure, have a seat." Brett said.

"Drinks OK? Need anything else?" Leonard asked.

"Everything's great. Brett here, is looking for his Grandfather, Garrett Arizona."

"I worked for the Danbury Mill here in '86 when they opened. Me and a few of the boys from work came here for a couple of beers and I met… uh, saw Garrett Arizona playing. There was a big crowd that night." Marty explained.

"Garrett Arizona. Yea, I remember him. That's been nearly twenty years. You said you're looking for him?" He asked.

"I know it's been a while, but we were hoping you might give us a lead." Brett said.

"I understand. I'll never forget Garrett. He came in one night looking for a gig to play. Said he was from

California and wanted to settle down. I tried him out on a slow night and boy did he bring them in.

We opened all the windows and all the doors and we went from ten people in the bar to over a hundred in less than an hour. Son, your Grand Pappy was one helluva guitar player." Leonard said.

"We were wondering why he left Pittsburgh? I mean, he wasn't here all that long." Amy asked.

"It was very strange. He came in one morning looking like hell. Said his apartment had caught fire. I don't remember too many of the details, but the Fire Chief's a regular and he said they never found out what started it."

"What happened to him?" Brett asked.

Leonard moved in his chair and then looked straight down at the table. He paused for a brief moment. The three could tell he wasn't at all comfortable retelling this story. "Well, when he came in, I told him to lay down in the apartment upstairs. Later that afternoon, one of the drummers, Jimmy Klein dropped by and grabbed the keys to Garrett's truck without asking." Hesitating for just a moment, he continued. "That's the part that's really sad."

"What do you mean?" Brett asked.

"Well, Jimmy had been in and out of prison and I tried to give him a second chance. Well, Jimmy was driving

Garrett's truck when he was trying to outrun the law. He almost cleared the train track on the other side of town but… he didn't make it. That's about all I remember." Leonard said.

Amy put her hand over her mouth. "Oh, my God!"

A sickening silence fell over the group. Finally, Brett spoke up. "Where did he go after that?" He asked.

"He left town. Last I heard, he was playing somewhere in Charleston, but that was a long time ago. We never heard from him again. That's all I know." Leonard said.

Before leaving, they learned that all the wreckage on the east side went to Three Rivers Salvage. Stepping out of the Tavern, the three walked toward the old truck. Marty smiled at Brett and Amy.

"You know, I hate it when I'm always right. I said Pittsburgh was a dead end and guess what? It's a dead end. But, hey, I'm not going to be the one who says, I told you so."

"Marty, you just did." Brett said.

"I'm just trying to make a point. We need to get back to the Motel and plan our next move. Which means, getting on to the next town." Marty said.

"Marty, I'd like to spend some time alone with Brett. Can you go get something to eat close to the Motel and we can meet up later?" Amy asked.

"Sure. I know I'm extra baggage. The third wheel. The tag along. The fly on the wall. The uncle who isn't loved. The…"

Brett shook his head. "Marty! Just an hour or two, okay?"

"Alright then, I know when I'm not wanted."

TEN MINUTES LATER they were back in the Motel room. Changing their clothes, Brett and Amy left Marty to watch TV. From the Motel's upstairs window, Marty saw them get in the truck and drive away. He went back to the serious business of watching TV. Pulling up to the bus station, Brett went inside and bought Marty a one-way ticket back home while Amy painted her nails happy in the thought of finally getting rid of him. Walking back to the truck, a feeling of guilt came over Brett for sending Marty back on a bus. As they pulled into the parking lot across the street in front of the Motel, Marty was walking back with two sacks. One full of food and the other hid a six pack of beer. All they had to do now was wait for him to be back in his room, write a note and leave it at the front desk with the bus ticket. After a few minutes, they saw Marty through the window of the Motel room. Not wasting any time, Brett ran across the street to the front desk. A minute later he was back in the truck. Starting the engine, Brett and Amy turned down an alley and disappeared.

Sitting in front of the TV, Marty enjoyed a cheeseburger and bored with the news, he changed the channel to sports. He couldn't remember the last burger that tasted this good as juice ran down his hand and landed on his shirt. Just as he was about to take another bite, the phone rang. With a mouth full of food, Marty answered the phone. "Hello."

"Yes, I'm the Manager at the apartment. You and your friends came by today."

"Oh, yea, sure." Marty replied as he wiped a stream of juice that was, at the moment, running down his wrist.

"I asked our maintenance man, Charlie, if he remembered Mr. Arizona in Unit 12. He's worked here since '75. If anyone would remember anything, it's Charlie..." She said.

Marty continued to eat his burger. He was eager for her to get to the point. To him, it didn't matter that his mouth was half full of food. "So, wha did ha sa?"

"He said there was a box in storage marked with that apartment number. Sure enough, it was still there. After the fire, they put the few things that weren't destroyed in a box. Mr. Arizona never came back to claim it." The apartment Manager said.

Marty swallowed just in time. "Do you know what's inside?" He asked.

"It has a few clothes, a bible and a letter."

"I'm glad you called. I'll be over to pick it up."

"It'll be here waiting for you." She said.

Marty choked down the last bite of fast food and walked straight to the front of the Motel. He remembered a cab sitting out front and prayed it was still there.

It was.

Outside, Marty climbed into the cab and told the driver to head straight to 1201 E Main. On the way over, he remembered he hadn't called his sister-in-law and was sure Brett hadn't called her either. Finding his cell phone, he dialed the number.

Finally she answered.

"Hello."

"Yeah, this is Phil from Sky High, the sky diving folks and I was wondering if you had every thought of…"

"Very funny, Marty. I recognized your voice."

"You got lucky, that's all." He said.

"Where's Brett? I woke up this morning and he wasn't here and his truck is gone." Sue asked.

"Well, after you called last night, I figured he might leave and that's exactly what he did." Marty explained.

A sense of worry and anxiety came over her. "Where are you? Where's Brett?" She asked while trying to catch her breath.

Not wanting to upset her, Marty hesitated. "We're in Pittsburgh." He said.

"Pittsburgh!" She yelled.

"Yea, Pittsburgh. He and Amy have the letters and they're determined to find your dad."

"Well, you just bring him right back! The three of you …"

Marty interrupted her. She was not hearing him. "Sue, he's not a little boy anymore. I thought I'd tag along and give him a hand."

"A hand? Marty, if anything, they need adult supervision." Sue said.

"I resent that remark."

"You listen to me. Brett's Granddad has meant nothing but tragedy to this family and I have no intention of that happening to my son. Do you understand?

I don't want him ending up like the rest of the family, just another head stone in some lonely cemetery." She said.

"I do understand. But, wouldn't you rather me go along and keep him out of trouble?" He asked sincerely.

"You? Keep him out of trouble?"

"I'm telling you, he's not coming back!" Marty said. "Listen, I'll keep an eye on him. I'd actually like to see where these letters take us."

"Marty, you get your butt and theirs back here right now! I don't have a good feeling about this." Sue said.

"Nothing's going to happen. I'll keep an eye on 'em and I'll call you every day and let you know what's goin on. How's that?" Marty negotiated.

Sue began to realize her son had made up his mind and it was fruitless to keep arguing. "Alright, but I really don't like this but, call me tomorrow and let me know where you are. Please?" She begged.

"I'll call you tomorrow." He assured her.

THE CAB STOPPED in front of Garrett Arizona's old apartment. Marty felt like a private investigator. He asked

100

the cab driver to wait. He knocked on the door of the apartment Manager.

"Hello there. You said you had a box for me?" He asked.

"Sure, honey. Here it is." The apartment Manager said.

She opened the door and handed him a box.

"Thank you. I sure do appreciate it." He said.

"Well, I hope it helps."

Marty gave her a fake smile and thanked her by shaking hands.

Climbing back into the cab, he looked inside the box, slammed the lid shut and muttered something to himself.

Despite wasting thirty dollars for a cab, Marty decided to take inventory of the box. Inside, there was a tee-shirt, a pair of old socks and a few other items of clothing that smelled like smoke.

"Geez! What a waste of time. Just a bunch of old junk!"

It reminded Marty of his stash of cigars. The box also included a small bible with the name Garrett Rivers written in the inside front cover and a letter.

Opening the letter, he couldn't believe his eyes. He thought about the cab fare as it was now pocket change. He was sure Brett and Amy would be impressed.

As the cab driver pulled back into the Holliday Motel, Marty reached for his wallet. He felt an empty pocket and realized what had happened. In such a hurry to catch the taxi, Marty had left his money back in the room. Asking the cab driver to wait, he ran into the lobby and went straight to the elevator which was in clear view of the front desk.

"Oh, Mr. Staggs! I have an envelope for you." The desk clerk yelled. "I was supposed to give this to you in the morning, but..."

"What is it?" Marty asked.

"I'm not sure. The other Mr. Staggs left it for you. He asked me to give it to you in the morning when you checked out."

"Oh,...uh, yea. Thank you." Marty wasn't sure what was going on. He opened the envelope and looked inside. It had a note and a bus ticket inside. Taking a closer look at the ticket it read, Pittsburgh to Williamsport'. The note was short and to the point. All he had to read was the first line, "We're sorry Marty, but, Amy and I..."

Realizing what was happening, he ran up the stairs to the room, panting like a dog in one hundred degree heat. Opening the door, he grabbed his bag and fake leather wallet and ran back downstairs.

On the second floor, he tripped and fell, hitting his head.

Stumbling out the door of the Motel, Marty ran toward the cab and jumped in.

He was out of breath.

The cab driver had only closed his eyes for a minute when Marty slammed the door and woke him up.

"Hey Man! You scared the hell outta me."

Marty was in a hurry and ignored the cabbie. "Here's twenty bucks. I'm in a hurry. Take me to…"

Chapter Seven

After staying with Jim and Irene for a couple of weeks, I decided to leave. I couldn't see just dropping in, leaving little Sue and then run off the next morning.

I felt it was only right that I stay a little while and help them make the adjustment. I knew Irene would make a good Mom and despite the fact that my brother Jim and I never had ever seen eye to eye, I knew he would make a pretty good Dad.

So, before I left. I told them that it was alright by me if they took little Sue in and adopted her as their own daughter. I told them I thought it was the best thing for her.

At first, Irene said no. She knew what I was going through. It was hard, very hard for me. But, after a few days she understood what I was trying to do.

Give the little girl not only a home but, some roots. A real family with a Mom and a Dad and a place she could call home.

I can't say I don't regret having to leave her. I have a lot of things I regret doing but, life isn't always fair. I know that more than anyone alive. So, I left my baby girl with some new proud parents and I went back to my music. I did that for nearly *thirty years and then something inside made me want to go to Pittsburgh to be near my daughter. So, I went back to my uncle's place in San Francisco and packed up my things.*

All those years, he was kind enough to keep an old leather trunk where I stored anything and everything that was special. Pictures of Noreen and our wedding, the first pocket knife my Dad gave me, things of that sort. I was even surprised to find that hood insignia from the James Dean car. Later on, I made a belt buckle out of it.

* * * * * *

BRETT AND AMY pulled up to Three Rivers Salvage. Expecting the place to be closed, instead they found the owner working on his race car. He was trading engines from one wreck to another when they walked up.

Fred Pindergast had owned the salvage yard for ten years. He loved cars and didn't mind the oil and grease. Walking toward the office, he said he'd be happy to check the records to see if the truck owned by Garrett Arizona was still in the yard.

Looking through three binders, he found it. "I'm amazed that it's still here. Shows the bed was never sold and the cab should still be in good shape.

Ok, here we go. It's in Row Eight, Aisle Ten. Let me write this all down. The license plate number is PK8 QN5. Not sure it's still on the rear bumper, but it might help you find it." He said.

"What color was it?" Brett asked.

"Color? Oh, sure. Let's see." Putting on his reading glasses, he looked deeper. "Says it's black."

"Thank you, Mr. Pindergast." Amy said. "We'll start looking."

"No worries. But, be careful. Lots of jagged metal in the yard. I'd hate to have to call an ambulance out here on a Sunday." Fred Pindergast said.

Sifting through the remains of a thousand dead automobiles, it felt like they were walking through a cemetery. It was a cemetery, actually. No headstones, just dead automobiles. After what seemed to be an eternity, they found Row Eight, Aisle Ten.

Row Eight seemed to stretch more than two football fields. Wrecked cars and trucks laid in the dirt, back to back. Walking slowly, Brett took one side of Row 8 and Amy took the other. They were near the end when they came upon it.

It was a 1981 Chevy Pickup. The front end had been torn away by the train and only the cab and the bed remained. The black paint had faded to the point where it looked like a mist of white fog covered the old truck. Staring at

106

it, as if it were a ghost, Brett thought of the violent impact that meant the end of a thief, disguised as a drummer. While Brett looked inside the bed of the truck, Amy went through the passenger side of the cab. With the exception of the original owner's manual, and an old screwdriver, the glove box was a dead end. Amy looked under the seat and found nothing but a pile of old music sheets. What a shame, she thought. They were too faded to make out the words. Inside the bed, there was nothing but a couple of old tires, a few pieces of wood and rope. Next, Brett looked inside the driver's side of the cab. Under the seat on his side, he found a tire tool and a pair of old gloves.

Before giving up on the old truck, he took one final peek behind the visor. That's when it fell out.

"Brett, what is it?" Amy asked.

"It's a picture."

"A picture of what?"

"A picture of a man and baby."

"A baby?"

"Yea, here. Take a look."

"I can't believe it's not ruined." Amy said.

"The visor must have kept it from fading." Brett replied.

"Who's the baby?" Amy asked.

"It has to be Granddad and my Mom when she was a baby." Brett reasoned. "It was probably taken before he took her to live with Uncle Jim and Irene."

"She was so cute." Amy said.

"Well, that is about all this truck is going to tell us." Brett said in resignation.

"Let's head up to the Truck Stop on the Interstate. I want to look at the map and figure out which address we should go to next." He said.

Struggling, Amy tried to close the rusted out passenger door. "Ok, but this door won't close."

"Here, let me help." Brett walked around and pushed the door closed.

Walking back to the front of the yard took more than five minutes.

"I can see how someone could get lost out here." Amy said.

"If we stay on this path back to the fork, it'll take us to the entrance." Brett said.

Walking by a wrecked ambulance, Amy heard a sound.

"Did you hear that?" Amy asked.

"Yea, it's probably a cat." Brett said. Amy was thinking of something bigger. "Pretty big cat." She said.

"Let's go this way. I can see the garage from here." Brett said.

Behind them a heavy truck door slammed shut. A shadow and the sound of footsteps disappeared out of sight. Stopping in their tracks, they looked around but, saw nothing.

"I don't think we're alone." Brett said.

Amy started to get anxious. "I know. What should we do?" Amy asked

"Let's get out of here!" Brett decided.

Brett and Amy started to run toward the garage when someone jumped out.

"Ahhhh!" "Ha, Ha. Ha. I scared you that time."

Amy punched him in the arm over and over. "Marty, that's not funny!" She said.

"Geez! What are you doing here?" Brett asked.

"You should seek professional help." She told him.

"Well, if it's isn't Lewis and Clark. Or, maybe Laurel and Hardy is more like it." Marty suggested.

"You scared me half to death!" Amy said.

"The question is, what are you two doing here?" He asked.

"We came here to find Granddad's truck before we left." Brett said.

"Let me see if I understand what has transpired the past twelve hours. I take you to the Old Mill Tavern where you find out the story of Garrett Arizona's truck. And, what do I get as a thank you? A note and a bus ticket home! To say I am disappointed would not be close to describing the mental pain and suffering I am feeling right now. Betrayal! That's what I call it!" Marty cried.

Marty's head was down as he kicked the dirt below the old pair of boots. Brett and Amy weren't sure if he was really hurt or, faking it.

"Marty, I never asked you to go. You insisted, remember?" Brett reminded him.

"This trip is about me finding my Granddad.

You helped us find the truck and I appreciate it. But, this is something Amy and I need to do alone." He added.

"Brett and I can call and let you know what's happening." Amy said.

"Ok, I guess I know when I'm not wanted. But, after I got the phone call from the apartment Manager this afternoon and I picked up a box which contained a letter, I thought for sure I would certainly add value to this investigation." Marty said.

Turning around, Marty started back toward the waiting cab. He didn't have to wait long.

"Marty, what are you talking about? What letter?" Amy asked.

"I thought that might interest you. You see, when you were planning your getaway, I was doing the real work. You see, while I was eating my double cheeseburger, extra onion, extra mayo, no pickles they make the fries taste funny, the apartment Manager called. She said they found a box in storage marked Unit 12 and I paid a cab driver thirty dollars to go get it. It had a few clothes, a bible and a letter of extreme importance which I now have in my possession." Marty said.

"Who wrote the letter?" Brett asked.

"What does it say?" Amy added.

"Not so fast. I need for both of you to recognize the value I bring to this road trip. You see, it's not the letter that's important. It's who wrote the letter and the picture I found inside it." Marty said.

"Ok, I give up. Who?" Brett asked.

"If you want to see what I have, you have to take me with you, but no more patriot games."

"Marty, I can't take it anymore." Amy said.

"Well then, I can just go buy a CD player with headphones." Marty answered.

"She's not talking about your taste in music." Brett explained.

"Well, what are you talking about?" Marty asked.

"Three people riding in a pickup truck doesn't work when one of the three takes a bath once a week." Amy pleaded.

"Then what would you propose, my queen?" Marty asked.

"The only way you can go is you taking a bath or shower at least once a day. And, you can't wear the same clothes all the time!" Amy decided.

"What's wrong with my clothes?" Marty asked.

"If you took them off, they'd probably stand up on their own. And, the cologne you're using is not masking the smell." Brett said.

"Who said I was trying to mask anything?" Marty said.

"You did bring extra clothes, didn't you?" Amy asked.

"Sure, I brought two extra pair of underwear." He said.

"Wow! Two extra pair."

"Boy, in five minutes, you two sure know how to destroy my self-esteem which has taken me thirty-four years to acquire." Marty said.

"Ok, I'll agree that you can come along but, you'll have to get some new clothes. I'll even pay for some new jeans and a shirt or two or three." Amy said.

"So, do we have a deal, Marty?" Brett asked.

"Ok, you win. We have a deal. Buy me some clothes."

"Now, show us what you found, Sherlock." Amy said.

"Oh, yes. The forgotten letter. Let's go for coffee and we can discuss it." Marty said.

"Fine, but I wasn't kidding about the clothes." Amy said.

The three stopped at Win-Mart and Amy escorted Marty inside and helped him pick out new jeans and a few shirts. Before leaving, she asked the Manager on duty if he would dispose of Marty's old clothes and if the store had an incinerator.

They did.

Inside the Truck Stop, Marty took a shower in an area reserved for truckers. Waiting in the restaurant, Brett and Amy looked at menus. As the Waitress poured a second round of coffee, Marty strolled to the table with a new sense of confidence.

"Oh, there you are. They said there were three. Would you like some coffee?" She asked.

"Does a zebra have stripes? Is the Pope Catholic? Did Martha Stewart go to prison?"

"Marty!" Amy said.

"I like your sense of humor. Alright, here you go." The Waitress said.

Marty watched with sheer delight as the Waitress poured him a cup of coffee.

"Ah, yes, the beautiful black nectar. Who ever invented coffee should have won the Nobel Prize. You know, I started drinkin coffee with I was twelve. Do you realize that means a combined twenty-two year love affair? If only my other relationships were as successful." Marty said.

Amy was starting to become annoyed. "Marty, what did you find at the apartment? She asked.

"Of course, my dear. The Infamous Letter!" He said.

"Who wrote it?" Brett asked.

"Someone named A. L. Beasley. The address is Oak Park, Illinois, which is basically Chicago." Marty said.

"Isn't Chicago on the list?" Brett asked.

Amy thought so but looked through the letters to make sure. "It is." She said.

"What's the date of the letter?" He asked.

Amy looked at the faded postmark. "It looks like 1986. He must have received it before he left for Charleston."

"You are a master of the obvious." Marty said.

"Oh, and it was never opened." Marty said.

"So, you opened it." Amy said.

"Yea, while you were buying my bus ticket, I opened it." Marty said.

"Maybe, he got it right before the fire and never had a chance to read it." Brett answered.

"That's a possibility." Amy said.

Brett looked at Marty. "Would you read it?"

"I'll let her read it."

Amy pulled out the old letter and began to read.

"Dear Mr. Arizona,

I am responsible for managing the assets of the Roth Family Estate.

Of her late husband's collection of photographs, Mrs. Roth has directed this particular photograph to be sent to you.

Sorry for taking so long in sending it as I had quite an amount of difficulty locating you.

Sincerely,
A.L. Beasley.

That's it." Amy said.

"Who is A.L. Beasley?" Brett asked.

"He must be an attorney or some kind of trustee." Marty replied.

Brett put his hand to his chin. He was thinking. "Amy, if we head to Chicago, what letters will we bypass?" He asked.

"Let's see."

"We'll be skipping … Charleston, Lexington, Louisville and Indianapolis." She said.

Marty shook his head and then looked at Brett. "I'm tellin you, the trail is cold on those four. We'd be wasting valuable time if we tried to hit all thirteen letters!"

116

"I agree. It's obvious that Chicago is our next move." Amy said.

"Wait! Marty, you said there was a picture." Brett said.

"Oh, yea. How could I forget?"

Brett and Amy studied the picture for a moment. It was of two men standing by a 1950's looking station wagon.

"Marty, who do you think these two men are?" Amy asked.

"Read the back." He said.

"Wow, it has a date. September, 30th, 1955. It says, Garrett Arizona and Bill." Amy said.

"Who is Bill?" Brett asked.

"Nobody I reconize." Marty said.

Amy just stared at the picture. "Hopefully, Chicago will tell us." She said.

After Marty's second cup, Amy suggested he take a third for the road. She figured it would take seven hours to get to Chicago. Turning onto the Pennsylvania Turnpike, Marty and Brett took turns driving while Amy tried to sleep. She couldn't.

At twelve thirty-five in the morning, they pulled into a Motel in Gary, Indiana and agreed they should stop and get some rest. They asked for a wake-up call at eight. Depending on rush hour traffic, they hoped to make Chicago well before noon.

THE NEXT MORNING, they drove to the address listed on Garrett Arizona's letter penned in 1993. They didn't expect any breakthroughs but, Brett and Amy insisted on checking it out.

They found themselves near the Midway Airport. The words 'run down' did not begin to describe the condition of the apartment complex. Out in the street, a group of kids played touch football. Their families were too poor to pay for expensive video games.

The trio made their way to the Manager's office. One of them wasn't happy.

"This is such a waste of time." Marty moaned.

"Probably. But, you never know. This could be our big break." Brett answered.

"There's the Manager's office. It's closed." Amy said.

"Of course it's closed. They have a twelve month waiting list of people wanting to live here." Marty said sarcastically.

Amy leaned forward and read something posted on the front door. "Back at One-Thirty." She said.

"The old, back at one-thirty routine." Marty offered.

"Brett, what do you want to do?" Amy said.

"I think I'll call the emergency phone number. We've come this far." He said.

Brett pulled out his cell phone and dialed the number.

An abrupt response came from the other end. "Hello, can I help you?"

"Hi, are you the Manager at the Midway Skyline Apartments?" Brett asked.

"Unit number?"

"No, I'm trying to locate someone. His name is Garrett Arizona."

"Is he a tenant?"

"He used to be a tenant back in '93." Brett said.

"Sir. Do you know how many people come and go here?" The person asked.

"I thought you might have some records."

"Records? Sir, we don't keep records. Sorry I can't help you. Have a nice day."

As they turned to leave, an older woman walked toward them. Having lived in the apartment complex since it had opened, she knew everyone. In fact, she made it her business to stay on top of the latest gossip.

"Who did you say you were looking for?" She asked.

"Garrett Arizona." Brett said.

The old woman had a faraway look on her face. "Mister Arizona. I don't think anyone here will ever forget him." She said.

"Did you know him?" Amy asked.

"Know him? I know everyone who has ever lived here."

"He's my Granddad and I'm trying to find him." Brett explained.

"I can't help you with that but, if you do find him, you must tell him never to come back here ever again." She said.

"Why would you say that?" Brett asked.

"A curse, stronger than any I have seen, has been cast upon your Grandfather. He is a danger to himself and anyone who goes near him. That is why he must never come back."

"A curse? You're joking right? You're not joking." Marty said.

"You would be wise to go home and forget about him. What happened here, I have vowed to never speak of again. Now, you have been here too long. You must leave before anyone else finds out who you are looking for. They are not likely to be as peaceful. Many here feel your Grandfather cast a spell upon this place and would like to see him pay."

As the old woman spoke, an older man approached.

"What is going on?" He said.

The old woman never looked at him. Her eyes never left Brett. "These people are looking for.., they are looking for the man with the spell. He is a relative of theirs." She said.

"Your relative has a dark cloud hanging over him. You must leave and I mean never, never come back!" He said.

The three hurried back to the truck and drove in silence for a few miles.

"Now that was creepy." Marty said.

"No wonder he didn't stay here long." Amy replied.

Brett was confused. "I've heard of accident prone, but..."

"But, what?" Amy asked.

"It's beginning to look like bad luck and Granddad became best friends. First the fire, then his truck gets hit by a train, then this." Brett said.

"Bad luck? It wasn't bad luck. Bad things happen to good people all the time. The woman and the old man are superstitious. To them, everything is an omen." Amy said.

"They probably found out about the accidents in Pittsburgh. Accident, fire, who knows, but she used the word curse. Superstitious or not, my Granddad had a string of...

Marty finished his sentence.

"Bad luck".

No one said a word until Marty changed the subject. "Hey, let's go get a bite to eat". After eating lunch at a nearby cafe, the three drove over to Oak Park.

IN 1835, Oak Park, Illinois got its start as a small frame house that soon became a tavern. It was one of the few homes between the fast growing town of Chicago and the Des Plaines River. The owners charged fifty cents for home cooking, and a soft bed to sleep in.

As they drove through Oak Park, the feeling of being in a small town reminded them of home. Parking in front of an old house, they noticed it had been converted into a place of business. No front yard, just a concrete driveway for clients in a hurry to have their problems solved.

Expecting a law office of some kind with a sign that read, A.L. Beasley, Attorney at Law, instead, the sign read, Stuckey's Print Shop.

To Marty, this place was going to be another dead end, just like the last one.

Knocking on the front door, an older man with white hair, white mustache and a white goatee greeted them and invited them in as if they were his very first customer. Inside, they not only noticed the strong smell of printer's ink, but like a hive, workers were everywhere, like bees making honey. Of course, it wasn't honey they were making here, it was the printed page.

Like his Father and Grandfather, Jonathan Stuckey, was a third generation printer. His Grandfather had started the business in the early 1900's. Somehow, his descendants retained the interest in the fine art of printing. Taking them to his office, Mr. Stuckey shut the door.

"I apologize for all the commotion. We have a deadline to meet with our largest customer. What can I do for you three?" He asked.

"Actually, we had expected to find a law office." Brett said.

"You're looking for a law office?"

"Yes. A.L. Beasley." Brett said.

"Oh, sure. Mr. Beasley. Very nice man. Before I bought this place, he had a successful law practice. I think he retired." The printer said.

"Do you know where he lives?" Amy asked.

"I tell you what, let me call my real estate broker and ask him. He should know.

He was the buyer and seller's agent.

If you'll take a seat, I'll get him on the phone. This won't take but a minute. Harry always answers his cell phone." Mr. Stuckey said.

Sitting on the edge of his desk, and with hands stained with ink, the legendary printer dialed the number as the three listened.

"Hi Harry, it's Jonathan. I have some people looking for the attorney who used to own this place.

Yes. A.L. Beasley.

Oh, he is…

I see.

Now, is that the one out on Old Pike Road?

That's what I thought.

Alright, I'll tell them. Thanks, Harry.

Bye.

Time really flies. Harry said Mr. Beasley is now in a retirement home." Mr. Stuckey said.

"How old is he?" Brett asked.

"I'm really not quite sure. He must be at least eighty.

He's now living in the Old Pike Retirement Home. Here, I'll write it down." He offered.

"Thank you, Mr. Stuckey." Brett said.

"My pleasure. Now, if you ever need any printing done, we're just the place."

"Thanks for your help. We'll keep you in mind." Amy said.

Leaving the print shop, Marty was beyond aggravation.

"Brett, please don't tell me you want to waste more time on an eighty year old man in an old folk's home who probably has Alzheimer's."

"Marty, we have to at least check." Brett said.

"You mean check his pulse. Ok, Mr. Beasley, you barely have a pulse. You have one or two days to live and oh, I understand, you can't remember anything because you're old. Thanks for wasting our time. Goodbye!" Marty said.

"Marty, it's less than five miles up the road. It would be penny wise and pound foolish to come all this way without seeing what he might be able to tell us. Besides, we need to find out who the man is in the picture." Amy said.

"Alright, I'm just sayin, we can't go off on any wild goose chase simply because some crusty old man thinks he remembers somethin. My Grandfather was not only crusty, he had Alzheimer's and he'd tell these wild stories. When I was little, I used ta believe him until the stories just didn't add up. And, when I reached puberty boy, did I feel dumb." Marty said.

"We don't have to spend all day with him, if we don't learn anything in thirty minutes, we can leave." Brett said.

"Ok, but if he starts telling any wild tales, I'll be makin an exit back to the truck. And, you two can continue your interview with Mr. A.L., 'Alzheimer's for Life', Beasley."

"Marty, you don't have to come with us. Just stay in the truck. Brett and I are perfectly capable of interviewing Mr. Beasley." Amy said.

"Oh, no! I want to hear what he has to say with my own two eyes." He said.

"You mean your own two ears." Amy said.

"That's what I said." Marty replied.

"Whatever!" Amy said in amusement.

THE OLD PIKE ROAD was actually a highway that went through the heart of Oak Park. In the early days, it was nothing but a dirt trail where wagons crossed heading northwest.

After leaving the business district where the Print Shop found its home, the Old Pike Road became a two lane black top where thirty years earlier ranchers kept their horses.

The drive was not only beautiful, it was relaxing, except for Marty's choice of music.

"Oh, man! Do I have to listen to that stuff the whole trip?" Brett asked?

"Brett, you need to appreciate new types of music." Marty said.

As the old truck topped the hill, Amy saw the large sign. "Ok, here it is. The Old Pike Retirement Home. This is a nice place."

"Yea, you check in, you check out, but you never go home." Marty said.

The Old Pike Retirement Home listed eighty guests. The term, guest, obviously implied they would not be residents indefinitely. The home was not your typical retirement facility. In social circles, this was a very upscale place to live when the hair turned completely gray and living alone was no longer an option. It had an excellent chef, spacious rooms, and beautiful grounds with large oak trees to bring welcomed shade in the summer time. Friday night was Bingo and no one missed that. Saturday was Family Night, when families of guests were provided a delicious meal. Sadly, the dining room was usually bare on Saturday nights as most families lived far away or were too busy to come and see their aged parents and grandparents.

Entering the upscale retirement home, they immediately noticed that every employee wore white. White uniforms, white belts, white shoes. Even nurses wore white hats. It looked like they had entered a Navy hospital.

As they made their way to the front desk, a woman approached them.

"Hi there, do you have my medicine?" The old lady inquired.

"I'm sorry. We'll find someone for you." Amy said.

As Amy spoke, a nurse walked over.

"Ms. Engels. Come with me, I'll get your medicine."

"Can I help you?" The nurse asked.

"Yes, we're here to see Mr. A.L. Beasley." Amy said.

"Oh, Mr. Beasley. He's out on the veranda. If you'll check in with the front desk, I'll tell him he has visitors today." She said.

They walked from the far end of the lobby to the front desk. The room was large enough and the ceiling high enough to pass for a church cathedral. Standing behind the desk, sat Beatrice Cove, a veteran caretaker of the elderly. There wasn't anything Beatrice hadn't seen and she was quick to tell anyone who dared to ask. At the age of sixty, Beatrice stood five foot nine inches tall and every inch of her hair was gray. There was something about her that spoke authority. Her height, her hair, or perhaps the way she stood like a general commanding an army. She was a woman who truly cared for the aged and had started when she was sixteen. After forty-four years at the same facility, Beatrice became the General Manager.

Amy, Brett and Marty stepped up to the desk. Beatrice was on the phone.

"Yes. Mrs. Johnson. Yes, I understand. But, we can't allow any guest to roam the halls without any clothes on. We have rules that must be followed. Yes, I know. I understand Charles is eighty-two but, that is no excuse. That's why we've confined him to his room. I understand. I'm sure he'll be fine. Alright, we'll see you this weekend. Ok, take care, bye, bye."

Beatrice Cove looked up from her desk and saw three sets of eyes staring at her. These were not the typical family members she was accustomed to. Most families wore fine clothes.

Men usually wore sweaters in the fall or tweed jackets in the winter. In the spring and summer, expensive golf shirts while the women wore color coordinated designer sets with matching hand bags in the spring and summer and colorful dresses in the fall and winter.

Perhaps these were newspaper reporters from the Sun or the Times. She thought. Beatrice was used to them. Earlier in the year, a scandal had broken that one of the guest was actually a member of the Italian mafia. The old man was arrested in this very lobby. This had brought on an onslaught of reporters from places Beatrice had never heard of. It wasn't until the old man was sentenced to life in prison that the Home went back to a place of relaxation and tranquility, words taken directly from the marketing brochure. The three who stood before Beatrice were an interesting lot, she thought. A man, likely in his thirties, was unshaven. He wore a sleeveless hunting jacket over a new shirt and pair of jeans. She wasn't sure why, there was no hunting allowed on the grounds of the retirement home. The other two couldn't be more than nineteen or twenty. Their clothing was simple, faded jeans and tee shirts. Obviously, they were infatuated with each other. As Beatrice spoke to Amy, she quickly realized that these were not reporters. They were common people on a quest to find a lost family member.

She made it a point to personally take new family members to see relatives on their first visit.

Today, she made no exception.

Beatrice directed them to the veranda which gave a beautiful view of the north end of the retirement home. All someone had to do in sales was take new prospects to the veranda and they were ready to sign. It measured eighty feet long, twenty feet wide, and forty rocking chairs, all of which made the veranda very popular among the guests.

Mr. A. L. Beasley sat in a white wicker rocking chair in the far corner.

For more than ten years it had become Mr. Beasley's habit to sit in his rocking chair after breakfast, lunch and dinner. He sat for hours smoking his favorite pipe reminiscing about the many fond memories of his late wife and his successful law practice.

At the age of eighty-two, he was in reasonably good health.

On most days, he was alert and could hold a meaningful conversation. However, A.L. Beasley had one major health defect.

"Now, Mr. Beasley suffers from a form of dementia. Fortunately, it's in the early stage, but his cognitive awareness comes and goes. Fortunately, his long term memory is crystal clear, but sometimes in conversation he becomes disoriented and completely forgets who you are." Beatrice explained.

"With him, it just takes a little more patience."

"Mr. Beasley." She said.

The old man looked up at the group with an innocence that only comes with age. His eyes were alert but his voice had the rasp of old parchment that was on the verge of crumbling at any Moment.

Mr. A.L. Beasley was a well educated man. His family wanted him to become a lawyer and make something of himself. He was small in stature, but his voice made up for his lack of height. Starting out as a trial lawyer, he became frustrated with incompetent Judges and juries. Because of the number of growing retirees in Oak Park, he soon found his niche in family estate planning. He hadn't become wealthy like his clients but, he had saved and invested almost every dollar he had ever earned. Such prudent behavior and discipline had allowed him to retire comfortably. He still combed a full head of hair, which had prematurely turned gray at the age of thirty-nine.

"Mr. Beasley, you have some guests who've come to see you." Beatrice said.

The old man looked up at Beatrice and a smile came across his face.

"Hello!" He said.

"Yes, Mr. Beasley, you have visitors. This is Amy, Brett and Martin."

"It's Marty."

"Mr. Beasley, they would like to speak with you for a little while."

"Well, Ok. Pull up a chair. Now, who are you?" A.L. Beasley asked.

"Mr. Beasley, my name is Brett Staggs and this is Amy and Marty. Mr. Beasley, we have a letter that you wrote to my Granddad, Garrett Rivers. It has a postmark, dated July, Nineteen Eighty-Six. He was a musician who went by his stage name, Garrett Arizona. We've lost contact with him and we're trying to find out where he is." Brett explained.

"I wrote your Granddad a letter?" The old man asked.

"Yes, sir." Brett said.

"Well, son, I wrote many a letter in my time and other than the Grand Canyon, I don't know much about Arizona."

As he finished speaking, the old gentleman's gaze, for a moment, became just a stare.

"We brought the letter with us, Mr. Beasley. Maybe that would help." Amy said.

Forgetting he had just been introduced, the old man looked at Marty. "Hi, I don't think I've met you. I'm A.L. Beasley."

Marty turned his head and rolled his eyes.

"Mr. Beasley, I'm Marty Staggs, Brett's uncle."

Ignoring the error, Brett handed him the letter to read.

"Here's the letter Mr. Beasley. You wrote it back in 1986 to my Granddad who lived at the time in Pittsburgh. Undoubtedly, you were handling an estate for someone with the last name Roth."

Taking a pair of thin wire rim glasses out of his shirt pocket, Mr. Beasley took the letter and slowly opened it with his large hands. Taking his time, he read it, folded it and finally, handed it back.

"Yes, I remember." He said.

"Mrs. Sanford Roth retained me to settle her estate. He was a photographer, you know."

"Who was a photographer?" Mr. Beasley. Amy asked.

"Well, her husband, Mr. Roth, of course. He traveled with his wife, and took countless pictures. He was an exceptional photographer. Best this country has ever seen, maybe ever will see. Mr. Roth even photographed many well known people. Well, he died in '62 and Mrs. Roth had some of her late husband's work published. When she passed, her will gave detailed instructions as to what would become of his work and his unpublished library of pictures. And, I mean to say, there

134

were a lot of pictures. That would be the reason why your Granddad received a letter from me and any pictures. He was probably on her list."

When he had finished speaking, he turned and looked at Marty.

"My name is A.L. Beasley. Who are you?" He asked.

Marty could not believe what he was hearing. His prediction had come true. The old gentleman reminded him of his Grandfather.

"My name is John Travolta. It's nice to meet you." Marty said with a slight grin.

The old man looked down. He tried to remember. "Travolta. Hmm, I think I've heard that name before."

Amy and Brett gave Marty a look that made him stop. They were learning something they had not known before and wanted more.

"Mr. Beasley, you included a picture with the letter. It was one of my Granddad and another man. Here, I brought it with me. On the back it says, Garrett Arizona and Bill. Can you tell us who Bill is?" Brett said.

"Well, let me take a look." He said.

"Oh, sure." Brett said as he handed the picture to him.

The old gentleman looked at the picture and then turned it over and read the back. "I never met him in person, but the man in the picture is Bill Hickman."

"Who is he?" Amy asked.

"Bill was an actor and a stunt car driver. Did you ever see the movie Bullit with Steve McQueen?" He asked.

"No, that was before my time. But, I know he was a famous actor." She said.

"I think that movie was made in the '70's. Brett said.

"It was 1968, to be exact. Other than McQueen, the movie starred Robert Vaughan and Jaqueline Bissett. Now she was a looker. The movie had a chase scene. Mrs. Roth shared that with me. Bill Hickman drove the black Charger that was in the chase scene.

Of course, that was a long time ago.

Mr. Roth died in 1986, the year I sent the letter and picture to your Granddad."

Without stopping to take a breath, Mr. Beasley looked at Marty.

"Sir, I don't believe we've met, I'm A.L. Beasley. Who are you?" He asked.

Marty looked down at the wooden floor painted white and smiled. Then he looked at the old man.

"Nice to meet you Mr. Beasley, I'm Osama Ben Laden."

"Nice to meet you, Mr. Osama." The old man said.

"Marty, could I have a word with you?" Amy asked.

Amy took Marty to the other end of the veranda. She wanted to slap him. "Marty! What are you doing?"

"Just having a little fun, that's all."

Amy wasn't amused. "That wasn't funny." She said

"He can't tell the difference. You heard what the lady said. His memory comes and goes, remember?"

"Just because he has trouble with his memory doesn't give you the right to make fun of him. You're being very rude and disrespectful. He's an old man who doesn't deserve to be treated like a child. Least of all, it's very distracting. And, he's telling us what we need to know." She said.

"Alright, I'm sorry. It won't happen again." Marty said.

"Of course it won't happen again because you're not going back. You can either stay in the truck or wait in the lobby until we're ready to leave."

"Amy, your sharp claws are starting to annoy me." He said.

"Marty honey, you haven't experienced sharp claws, yet. Now, go somewhere and let the adults talk." Amy demanded.

Marty walked to the front and waited in the lobby. He found a soft couch, a magazine and a game show playing on a big screen television. He knew boredom was just around the corner.

Amy walked back and sat down. Mr. Beasley had just finished telling Brett about his successful law practice. Brett looked at Amy who gave him a smile. He knew from the look on her face Marty would not interrupt them again. "Mr. Beasley, where do you think we can find Mr. Hickman?" Brett asked.

"Well, I don't have my records in front of me, those are long gone. But, if I'm not mistaken, I believe I sent some of the pictures to his wife in Memphis." A.L. Beasley said.

"You sent some of the pictures to Mr. Hickman's widow in Memphis?"

"That's right. Mrs. Roth had separated a lot of the pictures out that pertained to Bill and she wanted his family to have them."

As he finished speaking, he looked at Amy.

"Hello, I'm A.L. Beasley. What's your name?"

"Mr. Beasley, it's Amy."

Realizing they had learned just about everything they could from the old gentleman, Amy sensed it was time to go. Standing up, she shook the old man's hand. "Thank you for your time. Mr. Beasley. You've been very helpful but, we have to be going." She said warmly.

"Yes. Thank you, Mr. Beasley. You've been a great help." Brett offered.

Stopping at the front desk, Brett and Amy said goodbye to Beatrice. As they walked through the lobby, they saw an older woman sitting next to Marty. They were surprised to see her arm around him. "Isn't he handsome?" The woman said to no one in particular.

"Well, actually." Amy said.

Marty seemed amused. "Brett, Amy. I want you to meet Gertrude Morrison. Isn't she a peach?"

The old woman was looking Marty in the eyes. "I can't believe he has come back to me!"

"Excuse me?" Amy asked.

"I can't believe my husband has come back to me." She cried.

Amy was beside herself. "Your husband?"

"After all these years, he's finally come back." She said.

"Marty, what have you done?" Amy asked.

"Nothin! I was waiting for you right here when Gertrude came running over. She thinks I'm her husband."

"And, I'm sure you set her straight." Amy replied.

"I didn't want to hurt her feelins. Besides, other than my mother, no one has ever been this nice to me."

"Marty, we've got to go." Brett said.

"Alright, give me a minute to say goodbye to Gertrude and I'll meet you at the truck."

Chapter Eight

At the beginning of 1986, I found an apartment in Pittsburgh. Finally, I was off the road. I was also glad to be near my daughter who had married and by then had a son of her own.

I was grateful to Irene who told me her and Jim had decided to tell Sue the truth when she was old enough, that I was her father. Irene said Sue didn't say a word.

I hadn't been in Pittsburgh long when I asked Irene to contact Sue and tell her that I wanted to see her and the boy. Irene was nice enough to arrange for me to meet her for the first time since that day long ago but, then it struck.

The week before we were to meet, I came home one afternoon from practicing with a new band and my apartment was on fire. It was a total loss. Then, later that night, our drummer took my truck and wrecked it. He and the front of my truck died that night.

So, I took off to Charleston, West Virginia. I was told that a band there needed a lead vocalist who could play guitar. So I left.

It seemed that everywhere I went something bad started to happen. A fire and a car wreck in Pittsburgh, another car wreck in Charleston and Lexington *then, someone tried to break into my apartment in Louisville and died falling off the roof. Then, in Indianapolis, every tenant in my building came down with a terrible virus. It started when I moved in and stopped when I left. Many of them died.*

It was a long time before I knew why the fire started and why the drummer died in my truck.

Most of those years, I thought it was a string of bad luck.

* * * * * *

WAITING IN THE TRUCK under the shade of a large oak, Brett and Amy discussed their next move. Looking at the map and the addresses on the letters, they decided to head south on Interstate 65. On their way to Memphis, this route would allow them to make stops in Indianapolis, Louisville and Nashville. Places Garrett Arizona had written from in '90, '92 and '96. It would cause them to bypass St. Louis, Evansville and Lexington. Places, they agreed, were unlikely to reveal anything other than another tragedy.

For what seemed to be an eternity, Marty finally came out of the retirement home. He was grinning ear to ear.

"What is so funny?" Amy asked.

"I don't know. I guess I never knew how much I liked bein around the old folks." He said.

"You mean someone who thinks you're handsome." Brett said.

"I told you I had a way with women." Marty said.

"Alright, Don Juan, would you get in so we can get going?" Amy said.

Climbing into the truck, Marty was in an exceptionally good mood. "Ok, where we headed?"

"Interstate 65 south." Brett said.

"Wait! Hold on. That's the long way. Shouldn't we take Interstate 55? It's a straight shot to Memphis." Marty said.

"It's on the way to Memphis, but we can check out Indianapolis, Louisville and Nashville. We'll lose no more than a day." Brett said.

"I was right about Memphis all along. Doesn't that count for anything? You should respect your elders who've had more experience at this type of thing." Marty replied.

"What do you mean this type of thing? How many missing persons have you tracked down?" Brett asked.

"That's not the point." Marty said.

"That's exactly the point. We don't have to spend much time in each place, but we need to learn as much as we can before we get to Memphis." Brett said.

"The trail ends in Memphis, we'd rather not have to back track if we don't find him there." Amy said.

"You have someone in Memphis who can tell us where he is. What was his name, Bill somebody?"

"Bill Hickman." Amy said.

"Marty, why are you so interested in Memphis? It has to be either the Bar B Que or Graceland. Which one is it?" She asked.

"I'm only interested in Memphis because it's the very last letter." Marty said.

"Have you forgotten already? We learned a lot from Mr. Beasley." Amy said.

"Do you really think we'll find any more Mr. Beasley's?" Marty asked.

"Who knows? But, it's two against one." Brett said.

"Fine. I'm just trying to put my two quarters in."

"Marty, its two cents. You tried putting in your two cents." Amy said.

"That's what I said."

"Marty, you are a legend in your own mind." She said.

AS THE OLD TRUCK drove south on Interstate 65, Brett looked at the gas gauge. The needle showed empty. He intended to fill up before going over to the lawyers office in Oak Park, but had completely forgotten.

"We're almost out of gas. We have to take this exit or we'll be walking." Brett said.

"I could use the rest room." Marty said.

Amy pulled out her phone. She wasn't exactly a computer geek but, she loved to explore the latest technology. "Hey! I almost forgot. My phone has internet access. I can search Bill Hickman or Sanford Roth and see what comes up." Amy said.

"Good idea. See what you can find while I get some gas." Brett said.

"Go ahead, surf all you want. I'll be inside." Marty said.

Brett looked at his watch. It was getting late. "Make it quick." He said.

Brett pulled up to the pump and Marty went inside. Amy stood next to Brett as he pumped the gas. She searched online for Sanford Roth. Other than the fact that Mr. Roth had been hired to take still pictures on the set of the movie Giant, there wasn't anything new on the internet. What Mr. Beasley said was accurate. Sanford Roth had been a freelance photographer who traveled extensively. His famous work had been pictures of celebrities and a series of photographs of Italy in the 1950's. Inside the convenience store, Marty's cell phone rang as he walked out of the restroom.

It was Sue.

"Hello." He said.

"Marty! Why haven't you called?" She asked.

"I just called you yesterday."

"I've been worried. Where's Brett?" She asked.

Marty wanted reassure her. "He's pumping gas. Everything's fine."

"Are you sure?"

"Yea, I'm sure! We ran into some of Garrett's old friends. No earth shatterin news but, Brett's having a great time." Marty said.

"That's good." Sue said quickly then hesitated.

"Marty, listen. A man came by this morning and said he was looking for Garrett." Sue revealed.

"What? This is turning into a brush fire. Everybody's looking for Garrett all of a sudden. Who is he?" Marty asked.

"His name is.,, let's see, his card says, Dugan Sinclair."

"What's he want with Garrett?" Marty asked.

"He said he's an antique car collector and he's offering a reward for an antique collector's piece. I'm not sure what he's after. He thought Garrett might have it or know where it was." Sue explained.

"What kind of reward?" He asked.

"I don't know. He didn't say. I told him you were on a trip to see Garrett and he asked to speak to you so I gave him your number."

As Marty was about to hang up another call beeped in. Marty didn't recognize the area code. It was probably the furniture store. He was two months behind on his payment. He let it go to voicemail. As he walked to the truck with a diet coke in one hand and a six pack of beer in the other, Amy was in mid-sentence.

She had searched the name Bill Hickman and hit the jackpot. "Brett! Listen to this. Bill Hickman was an actor and a stunt car driver. He was hired to work on the picture Giant and became friends with James Dean."

"Who are you talking about?" Marty asked.

"I did a search for Bill Hickman and found all these links." Amy said.

"Read on, little sister."

"Well, Bill Hickman and a photographer were with James Dean the day he died. The two men were riding in Dean's station wagon and came upon the crash site."

"Wasn't he killed going 100 miles an hour?" Brett asked.

"Yea, he was drivin a fancy car of some kind. I think it was a Porsche. But, he died instantly." Marty said.

"Not according to this. At the crash site, Bill Hickman held Dean in his arms as he lay dying. He heard the last bit of air escape his lungs."

"That's gruesome. Couldn't you have left that part out?" Brett said.

"It says it happened on September 30th, 1955. That's the date on the back of the picture and it's also the day James Dean died in the car crash." Amy said.

"Granddad's in the picture with Bill Hickman the same day as the car crash, which means he was probably at the crash site." Brett said.

"Let me see the picture." Marty said.

Amy handed Marty the picture. Holding it, he began to study it.

"I didn't see that before." He said.

"See what?" She asked.

"Look at the bottom right hand corner. It looks like crumpled metal. I don't know, it's too hard to tell." Marty said.

"Hold on. Didn't you say there was a photographer with Bill Hickman?" Brett asked.

Amy stared at the blackberry for a moment.

"Yes, here it is." She said.

"Bill Hickman and a photographer named Sanford Roth followed in Dean's station wagon." Amy read aloud.

"That's why Mr. Beasley sent the letter and the picture. He took pictures of the crash site and some included my Granddad." Brett said.

Amy was still reading when she answered. "Correct."

Marty was confused. "Could you back up a little, I'm...."

"Mr. Beasley said he also sent pictures to Bill Hickman's widow." Brett said.

"But, listen to this. A great deal of controversy surrounded the fact that Sanford Roth had taken pictures of the James Dean crash site." Amy said.

"Maybe someone felt it was a little weird to be taking pictures of the crash site." Brett suggested.

"Weird ain't the half of it." Marty added.

"It says, that Roth stated in an interview that the photographs were taken for insurance purposes." She said.

"That's smacks of some kind of urban legend-conspiracy-theory." Marty said.

"Mr. Beasley said he sent some pictures to Bill Hickman's widow in Memphis." Amy interjected.

"That must be where they are." Brett said.

Amy had a smile on her face as the realization of their hard work had appeared to pay off. "And if we find the pictures they'll probably lead us to your Grandfather."

"So, it looks like Memphis after all. Listen and learn people. The cream rises to the top!" Marty said.

Brett and Amy looked at each other. Marty was right. Every clue led to Memphis. "You know, Marty, I hate to admit it, but you're right." Amy said.

"That makes one in a row." Brett said.

Pulling out of the gas station, Brett did a U-turn and headed to Interstate 55. If they drove straight through, they could make it in ten hours.

TWO HUNDRED MILES LATER, Brett was still at the wheel. Leaning against the

150

passenger door window, Marty was fast asleep when Amy interrupted the vacant noise of the old truck rolling down the highway.

"Brett. Are you getting sleepy? Do you want me to drive?" She asked.

"No, the coffee did the trick. I'll be awake for quite a while." Brett said.

"Good. Then, let me ask you something."

"What?"

"How do you feel about not stopping at every address your Grandfather wrote the letters from?"

"Well.., I would like to speak to more people who knew him and learn as much as I can. Who knows, he may have died and we just don't know it." Brett said.

"Something tells he's still around, somewhere. But, what I don't understand is, why your Grandfather stayed such a short time in just about every place he wrote from?" She wondered.

"In a way I want to know and then again, I don't." He said.

"I know, but, I have a feeling that we'd get the same story from every address in every city." Amy said.

"You mean we'd hear nothing but bad news." Brett said.

"I just feel something caused him or maybe forced him to up and leave every single place."

"But, it's obvious why he left Pittsburgh. A fire gutted his apartment and someone was run over by a train in his own truck. That would be reason enough for me to leave."

"I know. But, something happened in Chicago that was just as bad or maybe even worse."

"Like what?"

"I don't know, but, the woman at the apartment said your Granddad was under a curse. Didn't you see the fear in her eyes?" She asked.

"I did and I don't think she was joking." He said.

The thought lingered in their minds far longer than they wanted.

As they drove, Amy imagined the disappointment it would cause Brett if they didn't find his Grandfather or worse, if they learned he was gone.

While Amy was thinking about his Grandfather, Brett was thinking about his father. They had gone fishing the day before the accident. He missed him. The only thing that helped him get through it was his music. A few miles later, Amy wanted to change the mood. There would be no objections from Brett. She knew he never went anywhere without his bag and she couldn't imagine him going even to the grocery store, let alone a trip like this without his music.

She loved everything he wrote, but, there were a few songs that could lift her spirits when she needed it. She took out a CD and played one of her favorites.

"Let me guess, my music was calling you?" Brett asked.

"Do I hear a bit of conceit in your tone?" Amy asked.

"No, I'm just glad you like it." He said.

"I need a mood booster. You're very talented Brett." She bragged.

"I've been telling you that for a long time."

"I thought you said your talent was kissing." Amy asked.

"That's testosterone, not talent."

"Too much if you ask me."

"What do you mean by that?"

As Brett asked the question, Amy's favorite song, 'Gamblin Man' began to play. She was right. The song had an uplifting sound that could change her mood.

"What inspired you to write that one?" She asked.

"Marty, I guess." He said.

"Marty inspired that song?"

"Yea, he's always talking about his poker games. Hey, is he awake?"

Amy slowly pushed Marty's ball cap up and saw he was sleeping hard. She heard a slight snore and pushed the cap back down. "No, he's dead to the world."

"He keeps asking me to go, but, the guys that he plays with are all hillbillies. I can't imagine spending two hours with them, let alone five minutes." Brett said.

"You, mean they're all like him?" She asked.

"Just about."

Amy leaned against Brett's shoulder and went to sleep. A few hours later, they pulled into a Truck Stop outside of St Louis.

AMY AND MARTY both woke up as Brett shut the engine off.

"What! Whoa! Is this Memphis? I think I smell Bar B Que." Marty said.

Brett looked over at Marty. Somehow, he'd lost his favorite cap. His hair was standing straight up.

"No, we're outside of St. Louis. But, I'm sure the Bar B Que here is just as good." Brett said.

"That's because you've never tasted Memphis Bar B Que." Marty said.

"Marty, Bar B Que is Bar B Que. It's mostly all the same." Brett said.

"From what I hear, just saying somethin like that in the south would be cause for a hangin."

"Marty, what makes you such an expert on southern cuisine?" Amy asked.

"My folks lived in Memphis when Brett's Dad and I were kids. I must say, I've eaten a few ribs in my day."

"Oh, really." She said.

"Yea and, by god, before we leave the great city of Memphis, I'm treating you both to the best Bar B Que in the world!" Marty said.

"I can't wait." Amy said.

"I'm going inside. Marty would you top off the tank?" Brett asked.

As Brett and Amy went inside the Truck Stop, Marty filled the tank. As he put the nozzle back and closed the lid, his cell phone went off. The caller ID told him it was probably the Furniture Company again. He decided to deal with their pesky collection tactics once and for all.

"How many times are you going to call! I told the lady before I left town that I was just laid off and I'd make a payment just as soon as…"

Marty was interrupted by an intelligent Scottish accent. "Is this Marty Staggs?"

"Of course it's Marty Staggs."

"Mr. Staggs, my name is Dugan Sinclair. Your sister-in-law gave me your number."

"Right, Sue said you might give me a call."

"She said you were on a trip to meet Mr. Arizona. Do you know where he is?"

"Not at this point, I don't. But, when I do, what should I tell him is the reason you're lookin for him?"

"Mr. Staggs, I am a straight forward person, so I will be straight with you. Among other things, I am an antique car collector and I am looking for the original Medallion that belongs to a certain 1955 Porsche 550 Spyder."

"I'm a little confused. What's a Medallion?" Marty asked.

"A Medallion is a hood emblem, Mr. Staggs. Every original Porsche 550 Spyder had a number on the back of the Medallion that matched the serial number on the engine block. That is the only way the car can be identified as an original."

156

"I see. Didn't Sue also say you had some kind of re ward?"

"That is correct." Sinclair said.

"How much are you offerin?" Marty asked.

"Well, assuming that it is the original, it would depend upon its condition. But, at the very least, I am prepared to offer twenty-five thousand dollars."

"Really! Now, that's a lot of money. And, you think Garrett has it?"

"Precisely. So far, my research has taken me to him."

"What does this high priced hood emblem look like?" Marty asked.

"Well, it's unique, Mr. Staggs. It is about two and a half inches wide and three and a half inches tall. It is mostly bronze with an image of a black stallion in the center. And, circling the stallion are squares of red and black. You will recognize it, when you see it. There is only one Porsche Medallion."

"Tell you what, Mr..., What was your name again?"

"Sinclair. Dugan Sinclair."

"Well, Mr. Sinclair, I have your number in my phone. When I find out where he is, I'll call you. How does that sound?" Marty asked.

"I am counting on that Mr. Staggs."

As Dugan Sinclair hung up the phone, another rang. He recognized the caller. It was Remi. There wasn't anyone in his employ who he trusted more than his faithful assistant, Remi Cardone.

"Hello Remi! Have you made the transaction?"

"Actually, Mr. Sinclair, the meeting is set for three this afternoon."

"Excellent! But, I want to remind you not to accept anything except diamonds. General Ramirez will likely offer you currency. Whatever happens, do not accept it." Mr. Sinclair said.

"I understand. But, I just do not like the man. He is ugly and cruel. He kills women and children like it were a video arcade."

"Remi, he is fighting a war. We can't worry about what our customers do with the weapons we sell them. That is their business, not ours." He said coldly.

While Dugan Sinclair was taking the call from South America, Marty switched his phone to vibrate as Brett and Amy walked out of the Truck Stop.

He wasn't sure he should tell them.

Brett wasn't interested in money, and right now, the only thing he cared about was finding his Granddad and his music.

Marty began to think about his own affairs. He was laid off and his job prospects seemed bleak. If he couldn't keep the payments up on his place, he'd lose it for sure. Besides, Sue was a widow living on her husband's social security. The only other money she could count on were a few house cleaning jobs that paid little. He definitely wouldn't tell them just yet, maybe later.

"Marty, what are you doing? You look like you're lost." Brett said.

He was thinking about the money.

"Oh, I was just thinking how much longer to Memphis." Marty said.

"If you'll drive, I'll tell you." Brett said.

Four hours later, the three rolled into Memphis. It was very late and they were beyond exhaustion. Stopping at the first Motel they came to, the minute their head hit the pillow, they were fast asleep.

The next morning, it was almost noon before all three were ready to venture into Memphis. After a quick bite of a late breakfast, they drove directly to the address on the Memphis letter. 2015 Lewis Henna Drive. It had been from this address nearly five years before, in 2000, that Garrett Arizona wrote his last letter to Brett. Instead of an apartment, they found a two story house built in the 1950's. It had a large front porch and a balcony overlooking the neighborhood. There were no vehicles in the driveway, just a kid's bicycle in the front yard.

Standing on the front porch, Brett knocked on the door. There was no answer.

He knocked again.

As the three were about to walk back to the truck, an old sedan pulled up in the drive way. Digging herself out of the car, the large women, for a brief instant, just stared. Her face said she had never smiled a day in her life.

From across the top of the car, she yelled. "What do you all want?"

"We're looking for Garrett Arizona. He's my Granddad and we're trying to locate him." Brett said.

"Who did you say you were lookin for?" She asked.

"Garrett Arizona."

"Hold on just a damn minute. I need to get somethin." She said.

Leaving Brett, Amy and Marty in the front yard, the large women made her way into the house. The three looked at each other but, no one had an answer. Less than a minute passed and the large woman was back on the front porch talking on a cheap cordless phone. She could be heard for more than a block. "I'm tellin you, they're relatives of his, Bobby! Hold on!"

"Now, you three better listen and listen good. My brother is a Deputy Sheriff and I want you to leave." She said.

"Yes, but.." Brett started.

"And, if you see Mr. Garrett Arizona you can tell him the same. Don't ever come back here again!"

"But, why?" Brett pleaded.

"Son, what tree did you fall out of?" She asked.

"Huh?"

"Didn't you say he was your kin?"

"Yea." Brett said.

"Mr. Arizona is a nightmare!"

"What?"

"You heard me. Garrett Arizona makes any plague out of the bible look like a nose bleed. He's a danger to himself and anyone who gets near him. I can't believe he's not dead by now."

"Brett, we need to get out of here. If we stay, it'll only get worse." Amy said.

As they quickly made their way to the old truck, the woman could still be heard yelling. Marty kept looking behind them but, never saw Bobby the Deputy Sheriff.

Without saying a word, they drove down the Interstate a few miles and pulled into a convenience store.

"What was that all about?" Marty asked.

"Marty, did you do anything?" Amy inquired.

"Of course I didn't."

"Are you sure?" She asked.

"Why am I always the bad guy? Typical female. You can't hold me responsible for all your troubles."

"Marty, every place we go to, you're clowning around." Amy said.

"I didn't say a word. I swear. The moment we said his name, she went bezerk!" Marty explained.

"Whatever it was, she thinks he's already dead." Amy said.

"Are you rethinking what I said about bad luck?" Marty asked.

"Whatever it is, bad luck or bad Karma, we won't know until we find Garrett Arizona." Amy said.

"That sounds like an apology to me. And being the gracious person I am, I accept."

"Marty, that was not an apology. We need a phone book to find Bill

Hickman's widow. Would you go inside and ask for a phone book?" Amy asked.

"No apology, no phone book." Marty said.

"Never mind, I'll go. We need every phone number with the last name Hickman."

Amy went inside and asked the cashier to use their phone book. As she started to write down names and numbers, she saw a copy machine. After three copies and thirty cents, she was back in the old truck.

"Let me get this straight." Marty said. "You want me to call every number on this page with the last name Hickman and ask them if they're a relative."

"Yea. There's nothing hard about that." Brett said.

"There's more than fifty names on this page and my cell phone is almost out of free minutes. They'll charge me twenty cents a minute when I go over." He said.

"Would you rather use a pay phone?" Amy asked.

"No."

"Well, just don't spend any more time on the phone than you have to." Amy said.

"Right, like I'll gonna to talk about the weather. Hi, I'm lookin for Bill

Hickman. Oh, you don't know him. Say, what's the weather usually like this time of year?" Marty said sarcastically.

"Marty, shut up and start dialing." Amy said.

Amy divided the list of names between them. Marty was right, there were more than fifty names on each page. Brett pulled across the road to a park. There was less noise and they could separate and talk on the phone. Amy set on a park bench with her list while Brett stayed in the truck. Marty, set on a swing-set made for kids. After only ten minutes, Brett struck pay dirt.

"Yes, I'm trying to reach the family of Bill Hickman."

"Which Bill Hickman are you trying to reach?" The man said.

"Bill Hickman, the stunt car driver." Brett clarified.

"He's my uncle, but, he died in '86."

"Actually, I'm trying to reach his widow."

"She's not with us either. They're both gone." The man said.

"I'm sorry to hear that." Brett said.

"Why are you looking for his widow?"

"I'm trying to locate my Granddad, Garrett Arizona. We have a picture of him and Bill together. It came from a retired attorney in Chicago that told us he had sent pictures to Bill's widow. My girlfriend and I think that the pictures might lead us to my Granddad."

"I know about the pictures. The family decided that one of my cousin's should keep them. She's the historian in the family." He said.

"How can I reach her?" Brett asked.

"She's right here in Memphis. Her name is Doris Wellman. Hold on and I'll get her number for you."

Brett held the line and in less than a minute had her phone number and address. Hanging up, he immediately called her. After a brief explanation, Brett asked if they could drop by and speak to her in person. She was thrilled.

As the three climbed back into the old truck, Brett looked at Marty and smiled. "See Marty, that wasn't so hard". Brett said.

"You just got lucky, that's all." Marty said.

"Marty, luck is where preparation and hard work meets opportunity. By the way, how many phone calls did you make?" Amy asked.

"Two". He said.

"Two?" She asked.

"Yea, two. What's wrong with that?" He asked.

"You spent a half hour and made just two phone calls?" She asked.

"They were two very productive phone calls."

"You said you weren't going to talk about the weather, remember?" Amy asked.

"We didn't talk about the weather." Marty said.

"Then, what did you talk about?" She asked.

"Well, obviously, by the sound of their voice, I could tell they were two very attractive women and they wanted to know where I was from and I had to explain what we were doing in Memphis."

"You can't tell how attractive a person is just by the sound of their voice." Amy said.

"Oh, really. Well, how would you explain my first wife?" Marty asked.

Amy started. "I never meet your first wife and what does that have to do with anything?"

"Marty, your first wife wasn't pretty." Brett said.

"Who's your second wife?" Amy asked.

"I've only had one wife." Marty answered.

"You only say 'first wife' when you've had more than one wife." Amy said.

"Whatever, beauty is in the eye of the beholden. When I heard her voice over the CB Radio, I knew we were meant for each other."

"You know what, that is one heartwarming story. So, what did her voice sound like that convinced you she was so attractive?" Amy said.

"Well, I was drivin home one night after pullin a double at the Mill and I heard this sexy voice on the CB asking for directions and then…"

IN LESS THAN fifteen minutes, Brett, Amy and Marty sat in the living room of Doris Wellman, a second cousin of Bill Hickman. Her primary occupation was the buying, restoring and selling of used furniture. She had been in the business for more than twenty years. But, her passion was researching family genealogy and history. She rarely had an audience as there hadn't been anyone in the entire Hickman clan who was interested in the family's history. That is how it usually went. One person in the entire family is interested beyond words while the rest of the family had no desire to spend any time whatsoever doing research on a dead relative.

Doris was just the opposite. To her, it was uncovering history and even secrets of the past. She had only met him once but, she felt she knew Bill Hickman more than anyone. The stories her family had told since she was a little girl and the exhaustive research she'd done on her own had made her feel like an expert on the subject. To her, Bill Hickman was an exciting character in a family consisting of people no one cared about.

"Bill was very bright, but he lived life on the edge. I'm sure you heard about his famous chase scenes. Like the movie, Bullitt and, the popular movie The French Connection." She said.

"Mr. Beasley in Chicago told us." Amy interjected.

"Oh!, Mr. Beasley, yes, a very nice man. I spoke to him on the phone once. I had questions about the pictures he sent my aunt. He was very helpful but, unfortunately, he didn't have much time. He was moving out of his office…"

"Mrs. Wellman."

"Oh, please call me, Doris. I feel like you all are family now."

"Thank you." Brett said.

"Doris, Mr. Beasley sent this picture to my Granddad, Garrett Arizona, in 1986. It's my Granddad and Bill." Brett said.

"I recognize the picture. I have a lot of those." Doris said.

"You knew about my Granddad?"

"Yes, I met him at my great aunt's funeral, but it wasn't until Mr. Beasley sent the pictures that I really knew who he was. He introduced himself as a friend of the family and said he met Bill in California." She said.

"Doris, could I look at the pictures?" Amy asked.

"Oh yes, I thought you might want to see them. They're here in this box. Help yourself."

Amy sat down on the floor and began looking through what seemed to be more than one hundred pictures. One by one, she examined them, asked questions and then handed the pictures to Brett and Marty.

"Doris, these pictures of the crash, well, they're... gruesome." Amy said.

"Gruesome? That's nothin, look at this one." Marty said.

"Marty, do you mind?" Amy asked.

"Mrs. Wellman, what happened that day?" Brett wondered.

"Well, Bill and Sanford Roth were following James Dean the day he died." Doris revealed.

"We read that on the internet. They were following in his station wagon." Amy said.

"That's right. It was September 30th, 1955 and James Dean was off to a race in Salinas, California. They found Dean right after it happened.

The car was wrecked almost beyond recognition." She said.

As Doris began talking about the Porsche Spyder, Marty realized that the car she was talking about was the same type of car that Dugan Sinclair had called about. A 1955 Porsche 550 Spyder.

Marty picked up the pile of pictures and began looking for anything resembling a hood emblem. After more than twenty-five pictures, Marty noticed one that was different from the rest. "Ms. Wellman? Does that look like something in his hand?" He asked.

Handing the picture to her, she examined it closely through a magnifying glass. It was a photograph of Bill and Garrett Arizona at the crash site. The wrecked car was in the background. In this one, Garrett was holding something in his hand. As she leaned over the picture under the light of an old lamp, Marty thought about the description Dugan Sinclair had given him of the hood emblem. "Well, it's unique, Mr. Staggs. It is about two and a half inches wide and three and a half inches tall. It is mostly bronze with an image of a black stallion in the center. And, circling the stallion are squares of red and black. You will recognize it, when you see it. There is only one Porsche Medallion."

Doris looked over at Marty. "It does look like a piece of metal in his hand but, I'm not sure what it is, Marty." This was the part she enjoyed the most. The joy of discovering something that had to do with family history and, more importantly, anything that had meaning.

Handing the picture back to him, Marty looked at it closely. This time he was certain. It had to be the Porsche Medallion. Marty wasn't sure she would part with any of the pictures but, he decided to ask. He had nothing to lose, except for the twenty-five thousand.

"Could I make a copy of it?" He asked.

Brett and Amy gave Marty a look of surprise. "What could he possibly want with one of the pictures?" They thought.

"Oh, why don't you just keep it? Brett's Grandfather is in it and besides, I have more of these than I'll ever have any use for." Doris said.

Amy stared at one of the pictures. She seemed to be lost in a train of thought. "What I don't understand is how Brett's Grandfather got there. He must have been riding with Bill and Sanford in their car."

"I wondered the same thing. But, if you look at these pictures, he's not in any of them." She said.

"This one has James Dean standing up smiling, obviously taken before the crash."

"Are you sure it's September 30th?" Amy asked.

"It's not only the same day Amy, it's a picture of Dean, Bill and Sanford before they took off that morning. There are several photos of them before they left. But, Garrett isn't there. They must have picked him up along the way. That's the only thing I can think of." Doris said.

"Have you heard from my Granddad, since the funeral? Memphis is the last address he wrote from." Brett said.

"I never saw your Grandfather after the funeral except right before he left town. I knew you would want to know, but after that strange man came by a few months ago, I wanted to make sure the three of you were who you said you were, before I said anything." She said.

"What strange man?" Brett asked.

A man came by asking questions about Bill Hickman and the crash site. He had this strange look when he asked about Garrett Arizona. I told him I didn't know where he was. I wasn't sure Garrett would want me to say anything.

"What do you think he was after?" Marty asked.

"I'm not sure. He just gave me a bad feeling."

"Where did my Granddad go?" Brett had to ask.

"Well, a few days after the funeral, your Grandfather stopped by and said he was leaving town. He had a few pieces of furniture to get rid of and asked if I'd sell them. Then we'd split the money. I said I'd be glad to, so he left his forwarding address and I sent him about five-hundred dollars within a few weeks. That was four and a half years ago, and I haven't heard from him since." Doris explained.

"Where was the forwarding address?" Brett asked.

"I'll have to look it up, but it was in Sedona, Arizona."

"Arizona?" He asked.

"Yes, Sedona." Doris said.

"Did he say why he was leaving?" Amy wondered.

"He was looking for some peace and quiet. He said he had experienced more than enough tragedy in his life."

He must have been referring to Pittsburgh and Chicago. Amy thought to herself.

"He said that he finally came to understand the curse of the James Dean car." Doris said.

"Curse?" Amy asked.

"A lot of people died who had anything to do with that car. It's all over the internet."

"Are you saying the curse had something to do with Brett's Grandfather?" Amy asked.

"He said it himself."

"He did?" Brett asked.

"He said after the crash, the curse followed anyone who came close to the car or any part of it. It followed him for years and he finally understood its meaning."

"And, what was that?" Amy asked.

"As time went on, he realized that the curse differentiated between good people and bad." Doris said.

"I'd like to think my Granddad was a good man." Brett said.

"Your Granddad is a good man." Doris reassured him.

"Maybe that's why nothing really bad ever happened to him, only the people around him." Amy said optimistically.

"Like the drummer in Pittsburgh." Brett said.

"Wait a minute. If the curse only affected bad people, why did James Dean die if he was a good person?" Marty asked.

This was the part of what she did that made her feel important. Rare as it was, when she had someone who was interested in her research, she lavished the opportunity to share what she knew. "Honey, he died because he was careless. He'd already been stopped for speeding that day and he was speeding when the other car pulled in front of him. Bill told Garrett that few people really knew James Dean. Even though Hollywood created the image of him being a rebel, he was really a good person. Dean hated the greed of Hollywood and didn't care about money. He enjoyed acting and the money allowed him to do what he loved." Doris said.

"And, what was that?" Amy asked.

"Well, racing cars of course." Doris said.

"Mrs. Wellman, we appreciate your help, but we need to be going. I can't imagine how long it will take us to get to Sedona." Brett said.

"You are very welcome. But, would you drop me a line and let me know what's become of your Grandfather?" She asked.

"Of course, we'd be happy to." Amy said.

Before they left, Doris gave Brett the address in Sedona.

Chapter Nine

Over the years, I kept in contact with Bill and Sanford. I never had the chance to see them in person again but, we talked on the phone now and then.

I told them about the strange things that had been happening. They had heard about the so-called curse of Dean's car and they thought it was nothing but a publicity stunt.

I told them I understood but, that still didn't explain the bizarre events that I was experiencing.

But, what shook me up, though, was what happened next.

The band and I went to Chicago. I had been there less than a month when it struck again.

You see, I met a beautiful woman, not more than thirty, who lived with her mother in an old rundown apartment building near the airport.

One night, she came over to watch TV. When the show went to commercial I went to my bedroom to get a smoke.

That's when I noticed my wallet was gone.

When I came back to the living room, she wouldn't look me in the eye. She seemed nervous and told me she was ready to go home.

I cannot describe how bad I felt when not more than a few minutes went by when I heard a commotion. I ran outside and looked down the stairs.

She was lying on the ground all twisted and bent. Her purse had fallen and there on the pavement was my wallet.

That night she was killed when she fell down the steps after she left my apartment.

Her mother never could forgive me. She had the entire apartment complex believing that I killed her.

The police came and I told them what had happened. They took my statement which took more than a few hours.

Needless to say, the sun came up that next morning before it was all over.

That's when I began to look back and thought about the people who had died. The only conclusion I could draw was, if there were a curse, it went after the people who were evil or maybe had bad intentions.

To this day, I don't understand what possessed her to steal.

Maybe that was her intention all along. She sure was good at making me believe that I was something special.

*Sad to say, she learned the hard way
that I was special, just in a dangerous
sort of way.*

* * * * * *

AS THE OLD TRUCK drove west across the
wide Mississippi River Bridge, Marty
looked at the map. "That's what I'm
sayin. Let's drive all night and we can
be there in the mornin."

"There's no way I'm driving all night
in this truck between you and Brett
like a packed sardine." Amy said.

"Oh, so you're sayin I smell like a
sardine."

"I didn't say smell. Did I Brett? I
like sleeping in a bed. What's wrong
with that?"

"Keep me out of this." Brett said.

"To go on this trip, I've accommodated
you're sense of fashion and hygiene and
what do I get? More abuse." Marty said.

"Marty, I didn't say smell. You don't
smell like a goat herder any more, it's
more like a sheep." Amy said.

"Oh, thanks, that makes me feel even
better.

Now, would you do me a favor, please?"
Marty asked.

178

"What." Amy said.

"I want to look something up on your internet device."

"You want to use my phone? I don't think so." She said.

"Why not?" He asked.

"Because it's a five hundred dollar phone and it's taken me six months to get the internet settings right and I don't want you touching it. Besides, I want to find what Doris was talking about. She said the internet had a lot more about the curse of the James Dean car." Amy replied.

"I just want to see a picture of the car James Dean was killed in. The Porsche Spyder." Marty said.

"Fine. I'll look it up and you can see it." She said.

"Deal."

"Ok, hold on." Amy said.

Amy scrolled through several internet links until she came to one that said, 'The Famous James Dean Porsche Spyder'. "Here we go. There's an article about it with a picture, do you want me to read it?" She asked.

"Yea, read it." Brett said.

"Can I see the picture first? Geez!" Marty said.

"Ok. Here look at the picture." Amy said as if she were talking to a child.

Marty examined the picture from the internet. It was James Dean standing in front of his newly purchased Porsche Spyder. He could clearly see the Medallion on the front of the hood and was about to ask her to look for more pictures but, was interrupted.

"Now this is interesting..." Amy said.

"What's interesting?" Brett asked.

"Listen to this.

The National Auto Museum is offering a one million dollar reward for a piece of history, the car James Dean was driving when he died. The famous 1955 Porsche 550 Spyder has been missing for nearly fifty years. It vanished about four years after the fiery wreck that killed the famous actor. This is the first time the museum has offered a reward for any car." Amy said.

Marty was not expecting to hear this piece of information. "A museum is offering a million dollar reward?" He asked.

"That's what I just said."

"One million dollars, no wonder he..." Marty started to say.

"No wonder what?" Amy asked.

"Nothin. I was just thinkin." Marty said.

"Ok, here we go. Chuck Barris, he's the guy who created the Bat Mobile, was showing the famous car around the country. Then it says, after four years of accidents and mishaps, the car designer decided to ship the car back to California and…"

Amy stopped in mid-sentence.

"Brett, practically every one of these articles uses the word curse." Doris was right.

"Are you serious?" Brett asked.

"Yes, I'm serious. Here's one, 'The Little Bastard and The Curse of the James Dean Car'."

"It says;

After arrival to the Barris' garage, the car fell on a mechanic, breaking both legs. Later, a young teen, while trying to steal the car's steering wheel, severely gashed his arm. A man purchased the remaining tires was involved in an auto accident. The two tires, coincidentally, blew out at the same time. Soon after, the garage housing the car burned to the ground. Every vehicle inside was destroyed. Except one. Later, a man hauling the car on a flatbed truck was killed instantly when it rolled on top of him in an accident."

"Man. Anyone who touched that car was doomed. I mean one or two people that could be considered an accident. But, ten or twelve dying, that's no accident." Brett said.

"Amy, did it say why they called it the little bastard?" Marty asked.

She looked at Marty and shook her head. "When you went to the bathroom, Doris said Bill Hickman, the stunt car driver and James Dean became good friends while they both worked on the movie Giant. She said, Bill called Dean Little Bastard and Dean called Bill, Big Bastard."

"Oh." Marty offered.

"Remember the old woman at the apartment in Chicago? She said he had a curse. Then, that fat woman on the porch in Memphis, just the mention of Garrett Arizona's name and she freaked out." Brett said.

"Yes, but there's nothing that links James Dean's car with what happened to your Grandfather." Amy said.

"These articles are talking about the car back in the 1950's. Then, the car disappeared.

What I don't understand is why did all of these things happen to people who came in contact with your Grandfather more than fifty years after the crash?" Amy asked.

"Well, the common denominator is the fact that he came in contact with Dean's car in 1955." Brett said.

As Brett and Amy talked, Marty began to understand what Dugan Sinclair was up to. To him, it was starting to make perfect sense. The Museum was offering one million dollars for the car. Sinclair had said the Medallion had a serial number that could prove the car as the original.

If that was true, then a reward of twenty-five thousand was not out of the question. That, he thought, was a lot of money.

Marty imagined his next conversation with Sinclair. Getting the money from the Antique Car Dealer would be so easy.

TWO HOURS LATER, the old truck made it to Little Rock. Brett pulled into a gas station and a minute later they were sitting down, ready to order. The Waitress brought them coffee and menus.

Marty excused himself. He had business to take care of. Not the kind that meant sitting in a stall, but talking on the phone and making deals. Marty had never been involved in anything more than a few hundred dollars. This was different. If he got the money, he wouldn't have to worry about making mortgage payments. Not for a long time, anyway.

As he was about to call Dugan Sinclair, he thought of Sue and considered leaving her out of the loop. After all, he was doing all the work but, then again, she was the one that gave Mr. Sinclair his number. She deserved to be a partner, he thought.

She was a pain sometimes but, Sue needed the money as much as he did and he felt sorry for her most of the time. After all, she had lost her husband. Since his death more than five years before, she lived week to week barely able to make ends meet. Marty did what he could to help but it was never enough. If anyone deserved the money it was Sue.

Dialing her number, his conscience was healed.

"Hello?"

"Hi, little sister. I have some good news. We've hit the jackpot."

"Really?"

From the accidents to the million dollar reward, Marty told Sue everything he knew of the story of the infamous curse of the James Dean Car.

"Yea, that fellow Dugan must have found the car and is going for the reward. He needs the Medallion to prove he's got the original Porsche." He told her.

"So, how much are you going to ask for it?" Sue asked.

"He offered $25,000. I think that's pretty fair." Marty said.

"$25,000? All you're going to ask for is a measly $25,000?" She asked as if the amount was small change.

"Well, yea. That's more than…"

"Marty, what is wrong with you? You said the Medallion was the only thing that could prove his car was the actual James Dean Porsche Spyder." She told him.

"That's what he said, in so many words."

"Marty, wake up! Sinclair doesn't get a dime without the original Medallion. So, it's worth half the reward money."

"Half? That's almost…" Marty thought for a moment. The number rang in his head like church bells.

"Right, half a million dollars."

"Are you sure?" He asked to be certain.

"Of course I'm sure.

Now, do I need to handle this and talk to Sinclair myself?" She asked.

"No! I can handle it. I just wasn't prepared to ask for so much money."

"You call him right now and tell him how much you want and then go get the

Medallion." Sue directed. "It's that simple."

"Alright. I'll call him." He said.

As Marty hung up the phone, his legs became weak as he thought about confronting Sinclair. He had never been in any position to demand one thousand dollars from anyone, much less five hundred thousand. He had never seen that much money before. Sitting down, he took a deep breath and made the call.

Sitting a world away in his leather chair, Dugan Sinclair smoked a pipe while reading a newspaper. The smoke lingered in the air just above the small lamp sitting on the corner of his enormous mahogany desk.

As he started to turn the page, his cell phone came to life.

"Hello."

"Mr. Sinclair. This is Marty."

"Have you found him?"

"Yes, I've found him."

"Excellent! Where is he?"

Marty took a deep breath and went on.

"I'll.. I'll call you when I have the Medallion."

"What do you mean? I just wanted you to tell me where he is."

Marty's throat was constricted. He was more than nervous. "La..Look, Sinclair. I know about the re ward."

"What reward?" He asked innocently.

"Come on. Stop playin games. I know about the James Dean car, the Medallion and the one million dollar re ward." Marty said.

Dugan Sinclair became more than a little annoyed. "How do you know about that, Mr. Staggs?"

Somehow, Marty had found the courage to speak up. "It's called the internet, Mr. Sinclair and it's obvious you need the Medallion to prove it's the original."

"So, what is it that you want?"

"Money. Mr. Sinclair, a lot of money."

"Mr. Staggs, I have to answer to other people. Certainly, you can understand that."

"I tell you what. I'll call you when I have the Medallion and then we can discuss money. And, make sure you bring cash. The Medallion may be priceless, but I don't take Visa."

After Sinclair agreed, Marty hung up the phone and breathed a sigh of relief.

He had never attempted anything so bold in his thirty-four years, nor had he ever been under so much pressure.

Wiping a bead of sweat from his forehead, he walked to the restaurant.

Marty sat down as Brett and Amy were finishing their cheeseburgers. His food was more than cold.

"Where did you go?" Brett asked.

"I was on the phone with an old friend.

We hadn't talked in a while." Marty said.

"Marty, we ordered for you and now your food is cold." Amy said.

"Amy, my divorce has been final long enough to forget. Do you think this would be the first time I've eaten cold food?" He asked.

"Well, I'm glad to see you're not bitter." She replied.

Marty decided to eat on the way and asked for a to-go box. A few minutes later they were back on Interstate 40, headed west. Looking at the map, the three realized just how far Sedona was from Little Rock. This was not going to be a day trip. It would actually take them at least two days to get there.

FORTY-EIGHT HOURS LATER AND EXHAUSTED, the three rolled into Sedona.

With a population estimated at 11,000, Sedona was famous for its breathtaking rock formations.

Known as the Red Rocks of Sedona, the rock formations seemed to glow a brilliant orange and red by the rising and setting of the sun. Many came to feed their soul with the natural beauty as the red rocks created a stunning backdrop for everything from back packing to the more popular spiritual pursuits. The town was situated in a unique geological area that had mesmerized visitors for decades and was surrounded by red-rock monoliths such as Coffeepot Rock, Bell Rock, Cathedral Rock, The Mittens, and Snoopy.

The area was also largely influenced by Native American culture. According to local legend, the Yavapai Native Americans were the first people in Sedona and descendants of The First Lady, daughter of The Lady of the Pearl. The Yavapai Story of Creation recounts how The Lady of the Pearl was sealed in a log with a woodpecker and sent from Montezuma's Well at the beginning of the Great Flood. Legend recounts that for forty days and nights; the rain came and finally covered every piece of land on the earth. When the great waters receded, the log came to rest in what is now called Sedona and the woodpecker went to work to free the beautiful young woman. Carrying a white pearl, the woodpecker guided her to the Summit of the Mingus Mountain where she met the Sun who fell in love with her.

In time, she gave birth to a beautiful daughter who became The First Lady, mother of all the Yavapai people.

As the three drove south on Highway 89 toward Sedona, they were awestruck. Driving too slow, Brett caused a traffic jam behind him as he couldn't keep his eyes off the landscape.

"Brett, man, you're causing a traffic jam behind us. You're going to have to speed up." Marty said.

"How could anyone around here be in such a hurry? The mountains are beautiful." Brett said.

"I've never seen anything like this." Amy replied.

"Well, if he doesn't speed up a bit, by the time we get to Sedona, we'll have fifty angry drivers to deal with. How fast are you driving anyway?" Marty asked.

Amy looked at the old truck's speedometer.

"He's doing 35." She said.

"Brett, the speed limit's 60, you've got to go faster." Marty said.

Amy agreed. "He's right, Brett. You do need to speed up."

Pushing the accelerator, Brett could barely keep his eyes on the road. He had never experienced anything like the Red Rocks of Sedona.

Ten minutes later, they saw the arches. It was as good a place as any to stop for something to drink and figure out where Garrett Arizona lived.

Standing at the front counter to order, Marty had to ask. "Say, aren't the arches supposed to be yellow?"

"Yes, they usually are." The young man said for the third time that day. "But, the town council thought yellow didn't fit the landscape, so they settled on turquoise."

"Just thought I was losing my eye sight for a minute. I'll have a large coke and fries." Marty said.

"I'll have the same." Brett said.

Amy couldn't make up her mind. "I'll have a salad." She said finally.

"Say, where could I get a map of this little town?" Marty asked.

"I'm not sure, but around the corner is an area map on the wall." The young employee offered.

Sitting in a booth made of molded plastic, Brett and Amy waited for their order while Marty looked at the map.

"Ok, got it. It's on the far end of town. Thank god it wasn't a street with three names like, Bitch From Hell, which is the same street my ex-wife lives on."

"Right, Sunset Road is much better." Amy said.

"Brett, are you ready to meet your Grandfather?

I mean, you may have expectations that he may not meet. Do you have some kind of mental picture?" Amy asked.

"The only picture I've seen of him was when he was nineteen years old." Brett said.

"He might be a four hundred pound gorilla by now." Marty said.

"I'm saying, Brett may expect his Grandfather to act a certain way, but, then when he finally meets him, he's completely different." Amy said.

"I'm not expecting a saint, if that's what you mean." Brett said.

"Anyone who sings in a bar can never be a saint. It's like spaghetti. You can't eat any without spillin some on your shirt." Marty said.

"Marty, your metaphors and words of wisdom are…"

"I know. They should all be wrote down so that the rest of mankind can appreciate their timeliness."

"Marty, it's written down, not wrote down." Amy said.

"Listen cheesecake, words are relative. People don't talk in formal

English like they did in the 1700's. This is the twenty-first centry."

Amy pretended to be ignorant. "They don't?" She asked.

"No. That's only for the movies or English teachers. The rain in Spain falls mainly on the Plain." He said jokingly.

"Marty, what planet did you come from? It can't be this one." Amy replied.

Driving west to the far end of town, the old truck turned onto Sunset Road. The architecture made them feel as if they were deep in the heart of Indian Territory. Every home had the look of Adobe, with Burnt Orange, Turquoise, and a color that looked much like mustard. Pulling up to the older home, they sat in the old truck for a moment without saying a single word. All that could be heard was the sound of the engine running and a dog barking in the distant.

"Well, I guess this is it." Brett said.

"Yessir! This is what we came for, let's go." Marty said.

As the three stood on the front porch, music was playing in the old house. The front door was open and an old rusty screen door opened and closed as a slight wind blew through the house.

They waited for what seemed like an eternity. After knocking three times, still no one came to the door. As they were about to leave, Brett saw a figure coming toward them through the rusty screen door.

At first, he thought it was a child, until he slowly opened the door. It was an old Indian.

He was no more than five foot tall but had the body of someone half his age. His hair was as white as cotton and his skin the color of the sandstone rocks they had just admired.

As he opened the door, the three noticed his tan leather shirt and matching pants full of colorful beads. Marty thought the only thing missing was an Indian Headdress. He spoke slowly and with a deep voice as if his lungs were made of granite.

"Why are you here?" The Indian asked.

"We're looking for a man named Garrett Arizona."

The older Indian was John Henry. Now, a brother-in-law to the man they were seeking. To white people, he enjoyed speaking like an Indian on TV.

"Why you want him?"

"He's my Granddad." Brett said.

"This man you speak, he is my sister's husband. But, he is not here."

"Can you tell us where he is?" Brett asked.

"The man is on the reservation with his wife."

Brett gave him a questioning look. "Can you tell us where that is?"

"I can tell you or I can show you if you pay me."

Staring at the old Indian, Brett wasn't sure how to take him. "If you could show us that would be better.

We're not from around here. How much?" Brett asked.

John Henry looked Brett up and down and then spoke very seriously. "Two thousand dollars."

Surprised. Brett took a half-step back. "What? Two thousand dollars."

The old man stood there in silence. Then he started to laugh. Brett and Amy didn't know what to say.

"It is a joke." The old Indian said, as he was hardly able to talk.

Marty started to laugh too.

"Wait here and I will get my things. I would like to see my sister."

As he went back inside, Amy broke the silence. "Marty, I think we've found the only person in the world who understands your sense of humor."

"That's because you two don't appreciate a good laugh. I think the old Indian is hilarious. He probably wanted to pull that joke on somebody for twenty years.

I tell you, there's nothing more satisfying than making people laugh."

Amy smiled. "Then you must be very frustrated."

A few minutes later, the old Indian came out with a back-pack and a suitcase. "I am ready now." He said.

"I don't think we got your name. I'm Amy and this is Brett and Marty."

"My Indian name is Kicking Horse, but, I am called John Henry Clearwater."

"Ok, John Henry, how far to the reservation?" Brett asked.

"It is an hour by car. Three days walking."

Brett put the old Indian's suitcase in the back of the truck and after Amy slid in the middle, he offered the front seat to John Henry.

After shutting the door, Marty wasn't happy. Knowing he didn't have a choice, he jumped in the back of the old truck for the sixty minute ride to the reservation.

At least he'd have a great view of the scenery.

HEADING WEST, the old truck made the twists and turns slowly up the mountain. Leaving Sedona, the population grew smaller and smaller. Few people lived in the mountains. After what seemed to be a day in the bed of the old truck, Marty's back was thrilled as they made their way onto the reservation. This small community of people was part of the Navajo Nation, an area covering twenty-six thousand square miles of Northeastern Arizona, Utah and New Mexico. Even though the three had been expecting teepees, they were surprised to see real adobe homes. They were small, but practical and reminded them of a modern day apartment complex with no second or third floors.

There were fifty homes in the village and the old Indian took them to the very last one.

Parking out front, a dog barked and John Henry stooped over to calm it. As he stood up, his sister opened the door and greeted him. The old woman looked Brett, Amy and Marty over carefully and invited the four inside.

After sitting in the living room, she went to the back and returned with a pitcher of tea and glasses.

No ice, just tea.

John Henry took several minutes to explain who the three were and who they were looking for. She didn't smile and looked intensely at Brett.

Her penetrating gaze made him feel uncomfortable and he exchanged a look with Amy, who felt his discomfort.

Then she began to speak.

"Your Grandfather left when the spring flowers that fill the valley died. When the sun began to burn hot over the great land that became the lost prairie of my people and it has been more than two days since my husband slept in his buffalo blanket that stretches out upon the ground." She said.

"I never had the chance to meet him. He wrote me letters and I found them for the first time just a few weeks ago." Brett said.

"Do you have these letters?" She asked.

Brett pulled the letters from his backpack and handed them to her. Without reading them, she could tell by the postmark that the young man was likely telling the truth.

Finally, she handed the letters back. "My name is, Chases the Moon, but I am called Chase Rivers as I took the name of my husband."

"When did he move here?" Brett asked.

"Many years before you were born, he came here with his first wife."

Amy looked at Marty and mouthed the words "First Wife".

Marty smiled and mouthed, "Smart Ass."

Brett never took his eye off the Indian woman.

"She was a painter and wanted to paint the beautiful mountains of Sedona. But, that was before she died in an accident."

"I know." Brett said "He mentioned that in one of the letters."

"Her new life and her dreams were cut short. Your Grandfather was devastated and he buried her and then left Sedona." She said.

"I am impressed that you have come so far to find him."

Brett was beginning to get comfortable with her. "Can you tell me where he is?" He asked.

"He went to work on a memorial for the man called, James Dean.

My husband was there the day he died and it changed his life." She said.

"Where is the memorial being built?" Amy asked.

"In Northern, California but, there is something I want to show you."

The Indian woman left the room and in a short time, came back with a large leather case. She sat back down and took out a bundle full of pictures. "Since you are wanting to know more about your Grandfather, I think these pictures will help you."

"They go back many years." The Indian woman said.

"Thank you." Brett said.

Brett began to sift through the pictures and after looking at each one handed them to Amy who was just as curious.

"Brett, can I see them?" Marty asked.

Brett handed some of the pictures to Marty who had become bored with the details. Looking through the pictures, Marty saw Garrett Arizona on a stage performing.

He thought he recognized where the photo had been taken. He then turned it over and, sure enough it read; Old Mill Tavern, Pittsburgh, PA. Looking at the picture, Marty noticed an unusual belt and belt buckle. He couldn't make out the shape, so he leaned closer to the window where the light revealed something he had least expected.

It was the Medallion.

Obviously Brett's Granddad had made the Medallion into a belt buckle and was wearing it on stage. Marty wanted to jump for joy, but fought hard to suppress his enthusiasm.

"Excuse me, Mrs. Rivers." Marty said.

"Call me Chase". She said.

"Uh, sure, Chase. Umm, I have a question. Does Garrett still have this belt?"

"We come all this way and you're asking about a belt?" Amy inquired.

"It's a cool lookin belt!" He said.

"He no longer wears it but, it is the one hanging in the corner." Chase said.

She was pointing to an old antique hat rack that hung from the wall. It had an oval mirror on top and below four brass hooks on the bottom. On one of the hooks hung the very belt Marty had seen in the picture.

"Do you mind if I look at it?" Marty asked.

"It is yours to look at." Chase said.

"You break it, you buy it." John Henry said with a stare. Then he gave Marty a big grin.

"Marty. Before you look at it, can I see the picture?" Brett asked.

"Yea, sure". As Marty handed Brett the picture, he could hardly contain his excitement.

He nearly stumbled over Brett's feet as he stepped toward the hat rack. He couldn't see the front of the belt, only the side. As he turned the belt toward him, his excitement turned to utter disappointment.

The Medallion was gone.

Marty was devastated. His dream of easy money had vanished as quickly as it had appeared. "Is there a bus station in Sedona?" Marty asked.

"Yes, on Main Street." John Henry said.

"Why are you asking about a bus station?" Brett wondered out loud.

"This trip's been a waste of my time. I should have taken the bus back to Williamsport when I had the chance." Marty said.

"What are you talking about?" Amy asked.

"I'm talkin about you and Brett goin to California without me. This is your trip now, I'll just be in your way." Marty said.

"Is that what you really want to do?" Brett asked.

"Absolutely. I've got things at home to do. You know, big things, important things that can't wait.

And, now that you know where he is, you really don't need me anymore." He said.

Looking at his Granddad's second wife, Brett was glad he had met her but felt the need to move on. "I guess we need to get going. But, one last question.

Where is my Grandmother buried?" Brett asked.

"She is buried in the cemetery on the north side of the canyon." Chase answered.

The old woman told Brett that his Grandfather would like nothing more than to finally meet him after all these years. And, if he did not waste any time getting there, he would find his Grandfather at the James Dean Memorial.

The conviction in Brett's words were convincing, "There's nothing that'll stand in my way of meeting him."

The three got up to leave and thanked them both for their help. John Henry declined a ride back to Sedona as he had not seen his sister in more than a month.

"John Henry and I are very happy that you came. I hope to see you again." She told Brett.

Chapter Ten

It wasn't too long after staying for nearly a year in which we landed a high priced gig in Memphis on one of the Riverboat Casinos.

So, me and the band left Chicago.

I can't tell you enough how glad I was to get out of that cold town and I'm not just referring to the weather.

Once we got to Memphis, I rented a room from a woman I thought was pretty nice. She sure sounded nice on the phone when I called and I never would have guessed she weighed three hundred pounds. She said she had a room to rent and then went out of her way to let me know her brother was a deputy sheriff.

It was obvious that in a nonverbal sort of way, she was telling me I had better behave.

Well, her brother lived upstairs and the room I was to rent was next to his. She said his day job was law enforcement but when the sun dropped below the horizon, he was a dope dealer if I ever saw one.

One night, I got in well past four in the morning. I was as tired as a person could be.

When I pulled up, the house with the rented room was completely dark. I thought it was more than a little strange. The fat woman usually had all the lights on in the house.

So, I went around back and the door was wide open. Standing on the back porch I couldn't hear a sound. I stood there as still as I could when I heard someone from inside.

Whoever it was slowly walked down the stairs as quietly and carefully as they could. Since I wasn't sure who it was and not wanting to be seen, I leaned against the house away from the door.

Sure enough, a dark figure came out stepping ever so quietly. As he came off the porch, the light from the moon revealed his face. A face I'd never seen before. He was tall. More than six feet.

He had a bag in one hand and a gun in the other. Just as he was about to climb into his getaway car, someone fired from the back door hitting the man in the chest killing him instantly.

I stood there completely still.

When he turned on the porch light, it was the deputy sheriff. His right shoulder was bleeding badly and he fell to the floor and passed out.

I ran over and pulled him up. He was still alive. So, I called it in and in less than three minutes a dozen squad cars came barreling toward the house.

They found his sister inside. From what I could figure out, the man came in to collect a drug debt and met the fat woman who probably said something unkind. So, he hit her on the head and knocked her out. Then, he must have found her brother sleeping and shot him before leaving the house with the bag of money he thought was his all along.

The next morning, the fat woman came to my room and told me to pack up my junk and get out or she'd have me thrown out or worse if I didn't make it quick.

I asked her why.

In between the screaming and hollering, she looked at me with her nostrils flared and her eyes bulged out, and said that since the day I moved in, every enemy they ever had wanted to either kill her brother or run him out of business.

So, I packed up and left. It wasn't the first time I wasn't welcome.

* * * * * *

BRETT TURNED RIGHT out of the reservation instead of turning left, which would have taken them back to Sedona.

Marty looked at Brett. "You should have turned left. This is not the way to Sedona."

"I'm headed to the cemetery." Brett said.

"The Cemetery. Why?"

"We've come all this way, Marty. I just want to see it and then we can leave."

"I really don't do cemeteries very well."

"You can just stay in the truck. Brett and I won't be long and then we can leave." Amy said.

"Ok, you talked me into it. I'll wait in the truck while you two visit the dead." Marty said.

Making their way further up the mountain, the drive train in the old truck strained to make the steep climb. In ten minutes, they saw the arched gate of the Cedar Hill Cemetery which began as a resting place for the Indian Reservation as far back as 1863. Although the mountain was bare of trees, the cemetery was generous with cedars planted more than a century ago.

As Brett and Amy walked under the arch, they were amazed at the number of graves. There were more than five hundred dating back over 100 years.

"Man. This may take a while just finding her grave." Brett said.

Brett and Amy walked through rows of grave stones toward a tree more than fifty feet tall.

"Ok, it has to be here somewhere. Let's spread out." Brett said.

After searching more than ten minutes, Amy found the grave of Noreen Rivers.

She, however, was not been the first to find it.

"Marty, what are you doing here?" She asked.

"I got tired of waitin in the truck."

"Brett, here it is!" Amy yelled.

"Where are you?" He asked.

"Over here!"

"Marty, you said you were afraid of cemeteries." Amy said.

"I didn't say I was afraid. I said I didn't like cemeteries."

Just then, Brett walked over. He was surprised to see Marty. "I thought you were going to stay in the truck." Brett said.

"I changed my mind."

Their attention turned to the gravestone. It was a white granite headstone standing more than four feet tall with a name engraved in the center.

Noreen Rivers

Born   February 19, 1936

Died   January, 13, 1957

"You know, she died so young." Amy said.

"Brett, aren't you glad you made this trip?" Amy asked.

"I wouldn't trade it for a million dollars."

Marty was standing more than ten feet from the headstone when he thought he saw something and slowly stepped closer.

He could not believe his eyes.

The Medallion was staring right at him, embedded in the gravestone. For the second time in less than an hour, Marty had to contain his excitement.

"Don't you think we should be going? It'll be dark pretty soon." Marty said hurriedly.

"I'm ready." Brett replied.

"Me too." Amy said.

As the three walked past the gate of the cemetery, Marty pretended he had forgotten something. "Hey, I must have laid my cell phone next to the grave, I'll be right back. I'll meet you at the truck."

"You'd lose your head if it wasn't tied on." Amy said.

Marty ran back to the gravestone. He took out a Swiss Army Knife and tried to dig the Medallion out of the gravestone. As he worked the knife behind the Medallion, he thought Garrett must have used something stronger than mortar as he thought it would never come lose. Finally, it broke free and fell to the ground. Marty grabbed it, wiped the dirt off on his shirt and then ran back.

As he approached the old truck, the sun was beginning its daily ritual of dropping below the top of the mountain. The wind began to blow and the clouds turned dark. Reaching the old truck, Marty jumped inside barely able to catch his breath. "Alright… let's go!"

"Marty, what happened to you? You have dirt all over the front of your shirt." Amy inquired.

"I... I tripped and fell on the way back."

The weather was changing fast. As Marty ran back to the truck the wind picked up dramatically. The trees began to lean as the force of the wind pulled at the deep roots below

"Wow! Did you see that? The wind just blew that tree over!" Brett yelled.

"Can we make like a tree and leaf?" Marty said.

"Brett, he's right. We need to get going. It's getting dark really fast and I don't have a good feeling about staying here any longer." Amy said.

Brett pulled the truck around and drove down the mountain. He turned his headlights on as the sun had already set. "What happened to the sun?"

"Just don't run off the road. If you do, we'll go flying through the air to the bottom of the canyon." Marty said.

As Brett steered the old truck through the turns in the road, the rain started to fall. Turning his windshield wipers on, the rain became a downpour making it hard for Brett to see the curve in the road.

"Brett! Watch out!" Amy yelled.

"I see it!" Brett said.

Brett had turned the steering wheel just in time missing the ledge as the canyon was five hundred feet below.

"Take your time. I'd rather get to the bottom in one piece." Marty said.

"I know, except, It's not that easy." Brett said.

As the rain began falling harder, Marty looked out the side window and watched as the ditch that ran alongside the road turn into a flowing river. "Hey, this is not looking good. The ditch is full of water and it's running faster than we are!"

211

Just as Brett steered into another curve, a flash flood crossed the road and pushed the old truck into the ditch.

Amy put her hand over her mouth, not wanting to believe what she was seeing. "Oh, my god!" She screamed.

The force of the water felt like a Semi was on their bumper, pushing the old red truck more than a hundred yards as the ditch made a sharp turn to the left.

"Brett, the truck won't make that turn!" Marty yelled.

Brett struggled to maintain control of what now more like a boat than a truck. "I know!"

The raging water pushed the truck up the side of the ditch and stopped on its ledge of what now had quickly become a waterfall.

Marty opened his door and looked below. It was almost too dark to see the bottom of the canyon.

"Be careful! If this truck moves another inch, we're all dead." He said.

"Marty, this is no time to be joking." Amy said.

"Wanna take a look?" He asked.

Marty opened the door slightly and Amy leaned over and looked down. "He's right. If we move, we'll slide off the side of the canyon." She said.

"I'm not sure I can get it started." Brett said.

As Brett tried to start the old truck, the sound of thunder and lightning could be heard in the distant. For now, everything looked hopeless. Other than the sound of the rain, they sat in the truck in silence, having no clue how they would ever make it back down the mountain.

"Brett, how come nobody listens to me?" Marty said.

"What do you mean?" Brett asked.

"Well, I said it wasn't a good idea and guess what, it wasn't.

Unless you like to be stuck in a truck on the side of a canyon with no way out!"

"No one is to blame, Marty. Brett had every right to want to see his Grandmother's grave. If it were you, I'm sure you would want to see your Grandmother." Amy said.

"I never had a Grandmother." Marty reminded himself.

"Maybe not, but you would want to see her gravestone." Amy said.

"How do you know I'd want to see her in a cemetery if I'd never met her?"

"Marty, trying to reason with you is like trying to talk to this truck."

"Oh! So, now you're saying I'm as dumb as a truck."

"I didn't say dumb. All I said was…" Amy was interrupted by a sound coming from the rear of the truck.

"Crawl out of the truck. Help me with tow cable."

"It's John Henry. How did he get here?" Amy asked.

"I don't know, but who does he think I am, Indiana Jones?" Marty said.

"Brett, go help him." Amy said.

Brett crawled out the window, across the bed of the old truck and helped John Henry tie a wire cable to the back bumper. They both fought the rain that lashed hard against the side of the mountain. The one inch thick cable was wet and difficult to manage.

"Keep it tight. I winch truck back to road." John Henry said.

Brett held the cable while John Henry crawled back to his sister's Jeep. In less than five minutes, the old truck was back on the road and the three were more than relieved.

"How did you know where to find us?" Amy asked.

"When rain came, my sister was very worried you go to cemetery. She knows this mountain." He said.

"Thanks. Who knows what would've happened if you didn't show up when you did." Brett said.

"Been on mountain many times. Very dangerous. Evil spirits roam."

"Are you going back to your sister?" Amy asked.

"Sister wants me to go with you. Help you find your Grandfather. She has a bad feeling"

"What does she think will happen?"

"I don't know. Her Grandfather made good medicine for tribe. She has the same gift."

"What gift is that?" Amy asked.

"Is she a fortune teller?" Marty wondered.

"Sister feels sky. Knows when the will rain come.

After you go, bad rain came quick. She fears bad medicine on way to meet Grandfather. She says, I must go with you."

"Brett, can I talk to you?" Amy asked.

Brett and Amy walked a short distance up the road.

"Ok, I like John Henry. But, I am not squeezing in between a goat herder and an old Indian on the way to California." Amy said.

"Marty wants to go home, remember?" Brett said.

"You're right, but, we don't need any help getting to California. We just need to get down the mountain." Amy said.

"Alright, if that's what you want then I'll tell him we'll be fine." Brett said.

"Tell him we got this far and we're absolutely sure we can make it the rest of the way by ourselves."

Brett and Amy walked back to where John Henry was telling Marty all he knew about the belt and the belt buckle.

"John Henry, Amy and I appreciate your offer, but, we came this far on our own.

We're sure we'll be fine the rest of the way." Brett said.

"Sister says, I must follow in truck and watch for bad spirits." John Henry said.

"Are you sure you want to follow us in her truck, alone?" Brett asked.

"I cannot break my promise."

"Hey! I'll just ride with him. That'll give you and Brett more room in the truck. Who knows, John Henry just might like my kind of music." Marty said.

"I thought you wanted us to take you to the bus station." Amy said.

"Yea, Marty. What happened to, I've got things at home to do. You know, big things, important things, remember?" Brett asked.

"I changed my mind. That's all. And, right now, you couldn't keep me from going to California. Besides, John Henry and I have a lot to talk about." Marty said.

The rain had finally stopped and other than the mud, the trip down the mountain would be uneventful. Heading toward the bottom of the canyon, Brett steered carefully into a turn when he felt it.

"Damn! The tire is flat." Brett said in anger.

"Are you serious?" Amy responded.

"Yea, I'm serious. I'll have to get the Jack and change it."

"Where do you keep Jack? I can help change tire." John Henry offered.

Even though he had not known John Henry very long, Brett was starting to appreciate having him on this trip. "Behind the front seat. Let me get it."

"I need to make a phone call, but my cell phone can't get any reception. John Henry, where's the nearest tower?"

"I have sky phone."

"You have a satellite phone? How in the world can you afford that?" Marty asked.

"New Government Treaty." The old Indian said.

Having found the Medallion, Marty had lost all sense of timidity and was now ready to negotiate a half million dollar deal.

As Brett and John Henry fixed the flat, Marty dialed the number from inside the Jeep. After a few seconds, a male voice could be heard over two thousand miles away.

"Hello."

"Mr. Sinclair. This is your friend Marty…

Uh, correction, business partner."

"Mr. Staggs, we will become business partners after you have found what I have been looking for these past ten years."

"Mr. Sinclair, the eagle has landed."

"Excuse me?" He asked.

"It's one small step for yours truly and one giant step…"

"Mr. Staggs, what the hell are you talking about?"

"I've got it." Marty said.

"Are you speaking of the Medallion?"

"You guessed her, Chester."

"That is excellent, Mr. Staggs."

Dugan Sinclair was a financier and experienced businessman. To him it was highly suspect that someone of Marty's caliber, not to mention his level of intelligence, could have found the Medallion so quickly.

"Are you sure it is the original?"

"If I'm lyin, I'm die'n."

"Mr. Staggs, are you holding the Medallion?"

"I have it right here."

"Very well, would you describe it for me?"

Marty pulled it out of his pocket and described the hood emblem exactly as it had been revealed. When he was finished, Dugan Sinclair was still skeptical. After all, Marty simply recited the description he had already given him. There was, he thought, a fool proof way of identifying the Medallion.

"Mr. Staggs, are you still holding the Medallion in your hand?"

"Like a mother holding her newborn."

"Very well. Now, look at the back and tell me what you see."

"Well, there's an 'R' that's circled and a set of numbers." Marty said.

Dugan Sinclair shot up in his chair! He was not expecting Marty to even mention the fact that there were numbers on the back. He then reminded himself that Marty had learned about the Medallion from the internet. Perhaps, he was lying and there were no serial numbers on the back as he claimed. Dugan began to feel anxious that he was underestimating the man.

There was only one way to find out.

"Spectacular! Now, hold the line for a moment. I want to check something." He said.

"Alright, but I'm on someone's satellite phone. So, if we get disconnected, I'll have to call you back later."

"I understand perfectly. I'll only be a minute."

Dugan Sinclair was now intrigued. If Marty was lying, he would know it instantly. He walked over to his leather briefcase and pulling out a legal pad and found what he was looking for. Now, he was ready for this delicious moment of truth.

"Mr. Staggs, are your still there?"

"Like a bride waiting at the altar. Like a groom…"

"Excellent." Dugan interrupted.

"Now, Mr. Staggs, how many numbers are there on the back?"

Marty counted the numbers like a first grader studying multiplication tables for the first time. The delay only confirmed Dugan Sinclair's suspicion. After more than twenty seconds, his patience had run out.

"Mr. Staggs!"

"Wait! It's dark and I can barely read the numbers.

Ok, there's …"

The line went dead. Dugan Sinclair in a fit of anger slammed the phone down. He knew it. The man was a fraud.

"Hello! Mr. Sinclair. Are you there?" Stepping out of the Jeep, Marty forgot where he was and who was listening.

"Damn it!"

Marty only stared at the sophisticated phone.

"Marty, what's wrong?" Amy asked.

"Stupid… No good… satellite phone! Of all things, it lost the signal. It's a satellite phone! How could that happen?" He cried.

As Marty complained, Brett lowered the Jack and the spare tire came to attention. Now, they were ready. John Henry and Marty followed the old truck down the mountain on a rocky dirt road that had become slippery from the heavy rain. Brett took his time as he was determined not to slide over the edge and fall head first to the bottom of the canyon. Whether it was his nerves or he was simply in the mood, Marty talked non-stop while John Henry listened. "Thank god the rain stopped or we'd never make it down this mountain."

"God has nothing to do with it. It is a low pressure system. We are not out of danger."

Turning his head to face the Indian, Marty was not expecting bad news. "We're not?"

"Mountain has many moods." The old Indian enjoyed Marty's fear.

"You mean besides low pressure systems? I don't need any more stress. My hair is falling out faster than my head can grow it."

He looked over at John Henry. Marty was more than jealous that the old Indian had a full head of hair, white notwithstanding.

"What is it with you Indians? I've never seen one of you with a receding hair line. Bald maybe, but, I've never seen a widow's peek on an Indian."

"White man's way is reason you lose hair. White man greedy. Never sit on earth or listen to song of flute." He said.

"John Henry, with all due respect, that is the nuttiest thing I have ever heard."

John Henry steered the Jeep slowly down the Mountain. Up ahead, he could see the bright red lights of the old truck's tail lights come alive as Brett came to a stop. John Henry rolled his window down and saw a herd of mountain goats. More than a hundred mountain goats crossed single file in front of Brett's truck. Most had a tan coat with a dark brown collar around they're neck. Waiting for the goats to pass, Brett turned his engine off and the bright glow of the red tail lights disappeared.

As John Henry turned the key to kill his engine, the mountain came alive. The ground began to tremble slightly as the rumble brought rocks down the mountain. Hitting the side of the Jeep, Marty sprang to life. "Whoa! What was that?" He asked.

"Mountain not smile."

Above their head, the sound of thunder was heard. This time it wasn't an angry sky, it was the mountain.

Marty looked up and did not like what he saw. "Hey, we need to get outta here. Like now!"

As the last of the herd crossed the muddy road, Brett started the old truck and drove on. Starting his engine, John Henry pulled the Jeep into drive as they heard a deafening sound.

"Let's go! Let's go!" Marty yelled.

It was too late. Two boulders, the size of large barrels slammed into the side of the Jeep. The force crushed the passenger side and threw Marty on top of John Henry. "Move over, I cannot breathe." He said.

Marty moved back into the passenger seat.

"We must get off mountain now, before rain comes."

"Before what?" Marty asked.

The Indian looked out the smashed passenger window as the mountain came alive again. Marty looked toward the mountain and saw a wall of mud coming toward them. Scrambling to the back seat, Marty felt the force of the mud turn the Jeep onto its side. As the mud subsided, the Jeep came to rest right at the edge.

Marty crawled out the passenger window and yelled back at John Henry. "John Henry! You ok?"

Marty listened. He couldn't hear anything. "Hey, can you hear me?

"You are as loud as buffalo herd." John Henry said.

"The ledge is giving way. We don't have much time!" Marty yelled.

John Henry's head appeared in the passenger window and Marty pulled him up onto what was now the roof of the Jeep. The smashed four-wheeler started teetering as more of the ledge broke way. In desperation, the two men jumped onto solid ground as the ledge totally gave way and the Jeep disappeared into the chasm below. They were amazed that they had escaped a violent death.

Brett and Amy stopped and ran over to the ledge where the Jeep had disappeared. As the four peered into the blackness below, she put her arms around them both. "Are you two all right?"

"We did better than the Jeep." Marty said.

"You're sister won't be happy." Brett said.

"Sister make big smile, she wants HUMMER."

Climbing into the pickup, they started down the mountain.

As they made it to the valley to the north, the sky cleared and the stars came out.

No one said a word as they drove into the night headed to the James Dean Memorial.

Chapter Eleven

Music had been a big part of my life for more than fifty years and one day, sitting in a small café in downtown Memphis I stared at pictures of Elvis on the wall.

Most were from the fifties and sixties when he was much younger. He looked grand. He wore a white jump suite with a large collar that went halfway up his neck. Diamonds everywhere. His hair was combed back and he was as confident as ever. There wasn't any question in my mind that he was the indisputable King of Rock-N-Roll.

But then, the last picture on the wall was a picture of him in the seventies. He was getting older. Gaining a lot of weight, he had become only a shadow of his former glory.

As I couldn't help thinking about a lot of musicians I knew who played until they dropped dead, I started to realize it was my time to get off the road and finally settle down somewhere. Of course, I'd never stop playing my music. I could never do that yet, I simply was tired of moving from place to place.

I was also tired of seeing one tragedy after another unfold. For me, death had become the common cold.

Thinking of the best place to retire, I decided to go back to the place I loved the most.

I knew I'd be haunted by my wife's memory but, I was never more comfortable in all the places I've been than in the northern part of Arizona. It was a special place that Noreen loved and I guess that is why I had loved it too.

So, in late 2000, I packed up, said goodbye to the band and took off for Sedona.

After three days of traveling, I finally made it to the Red Rock region and I quickly realized how much I'd missed this little town.

It's one of the few places where you just couldn't keep your eyes off the scenery. It is that beautiful.

That's how the locals know how to spot a tourist. They're always looking up at the mountains. I can't say that I blame them.

After staying in a small Motel on the outside of town for a few days, I ran into an old Indian I'd known back when Noreen and I had lived in Sedona.

His name was John Henry Clearwater.

He had left the reservation and married a white woman who had an antique shop. She had passed and he was now living alone in her place.

It didn't take long to bring me up to date on the happenings of the town. Not much had changed.

What did interest me was John Henry's sister. Her name was Chase and she still lived on the Indian reservation.

* * * * * *

BRETT PULLED into a Truck Stop in Kingman.

Sitting in a corner booth with a full view of the Interstate, everyone ordered coffee except Amy who planned a night of sleep.

"Tell her to wait till I get back to fill my cup, I'll only be a minute." Marty said.

Marty walked toward the small gift shop to make a phone call.

Amy crossed her arms and appeared to be cold. "I'm still shaking. I can't believe what's been happening to us." Amy said.

"No reason for Brett to give up." John Henry said.

"That's what I was just thinking." Brett said.

"Good to seek out council of Grandfather.

He can guide you on path of life."

Brett thought about his Granddad. He had become used to the idea of finally meeting him. "You've got a point."

"Does Brett sing like Grandfather?"

"Well, I'm trying to. It's what I love to do."

"Your Grandfather song, great magic."

"I'd love to hear his music." Brett said.

Standing in the corner of the gift shop, Marty listened to his cell phone.

"But, it keeps going to voicemail. Why aren't you picking up?"

"Sue, we're out in the middle of nowhere, that's why."

"Is Brett Ok?" She asked.

"Brett's fine. It's me you should be worried about."

"What's wrong with you?"

"Nothing, it's been a hectic day. I have the Medallion."

"You do? Where did you find it?"

"Garrett put it on your mother's gravestone."

"Why would he do that?" She asked.

"I have no idea. I've got to call Sinclair, I had him on the phone and then I lost the signal." Marty said.

"Does anyone else know about it?"

"Hell no!"

"Good, the less anybody knows the better."

There was a brief silence. Both were thinking.

"Did you tell Sinclair what you wanted?"

"Aren't you listening? I had him on the phone and I lost the signal. I gotta go, I'll call you tomorrow."

"Ok but, remember, we want half the reward. I won't take a penny less. Do you hear me?"

"Little sister, you're preaching to the choir. I'll call you tomorrow."

Marty hung up and immediately looked through his call list to find Sinclair's number. In no time, his phone was ringing.

"Sinclair, here."

"It's me, Marty."

"Mr. Staggs, your phone calls are starting to annoy me. Let's make this one the last, shall we?"

"Hey, I was about to give you the numbers when I lost the signal." Marty explained.

"Alright, I'll give you one more chance, but, if you're wasting my time, this will be the last call."

"I have the numbers. They're right here on the back of the Medallion."

"Then let's hear them."

"Ok, here they are: 13HSR197DQ0531."

Alone in his library with the smell of fresh tobacco in the air, Dugan Sinclair sat in his chair chewing on the end of his favorite pipe. The man on the other end of the line who he had never met had given him the correct serial number and for the first time in ten years, he realized his search was over.

"Hey, are you there?" Marty asked.

"I am here, Mr. Staggs. You are a very lucky man. You have the correct numbers."

"Of course I do.

Now, listen. Here's what we want."

"When you say we, who are you referring to, Mr. Staggs?"

"Sue. We're partners in this."

"Alright, what do you and your partner want?"

"We want half the reward money and not a penny less."

Dugan Sinclair laughed. He had underestimated the illiterate man. "Half! Did you say half?"

"Yessir. That's what I said. We want half and not a penny less."

"Mr. Staggs, do you have any idea the amount of money I have gone through and the time I have invested, to be able to even have this conversation with you? Now, I might consider, assuming the Medallion is in adequate condition, one hundred thousand."

"I don't care if you've lost your arms and legs to get here, we won't take any less because you can't authentizise the James Dean car without the hood emblem. So, stop takin me and my sister-in-law for ignorant fools."

"Mr. Staggs, if you do not produce the Medallion, you will wish we had never met.

Now, where are you?" Sinclair asked.

"Not so fast. I'll call you when I'm ready.

Just make sure you have the money."

"Money is not the issue, Mr. Staggs, producing the Medallion is. And, by the way, the word is authenticate."

Visibly upset, he picked up a paper weight from his desk and hurled it across the room, completely destroying a five thousand dollar lamp. Speaking to an empty room, Sinclair was furious. "That little worm has no idea who he's dealing with!"

Outside the office, he heard the sound of a struggle followed by a sharp knock on the door. Still angry from the phone call with Marty, Sinclair spoke to the door.

"What do you want?" He asked.

"Mr. Sinclair, we have an emergency."

"Alright, come in."

An assistant and three bodyguards dragged a man into the room and threw him into a chair. The man was in his thirties and had worked for Sinclair a short time. Little did he know, his employment was about to end.

"This is all a mistake! I was just doing my job." The man said.

"We caught him downloading secret files." The assistant said.

"Tell me what you were doing or you won't leave this room standing up."

"It was only routine computer maintenance. I swear. Please."

"Mr. Sinclair, we checked his email.

He's had contact with Omar Haddid." The assistant said.

"So, you allow me to pay you while you talk to my enemies?" Dugan Sinclair asked.

"I swear. It's all a mistake." The man screamed.

"I agree, a mistake you have become."

Opening a hidden drawer, Sinclair pulled out a 9 Millimeter Smith & Wesson. Slowly, yet carefully, Sinclair pointed the gun at the man.

"Wait...No...Please..." Cried the guilty man.

Without hesitation, Sinclair fired hitting him squarely between the eyes. The man collapsed backward onto the chair as blood oozed from the fresh wound. "Now, get him out of here!" He yelled.

The bodyguards immediately dragged the traitor out of the room.

Calming himself, Sinclair walked to the window. Down below, two young beauties bathed in the bright sunlight by the pool. Seeing him, one of them waved. He motioned for her to come up and she grabbed a towel and ran upstairs.

INSIDE THE RESTAURANT of the Truck Stop, the four decided to continue driving instead of stopping for the night. They were almost to the truck when Marty grabbed Brett's arm. "Brett, can I speak to you and Amy, Uno Momento?"

"I can take hint. John Henry can wait." He said.

"What's up?" Brett asked.

"Brett, I rode up to the reservation in the back of the truck and it just about killed me. I ain't ridin all the way to California sitting in the back of the truck like that. My thirty-four year old back won't take it."

"Marty, he's in his seventies." Amy said.

"Indians like sitting on the floor, remember?" Marty reminded them.

"You watch too many movies". Amy said.

Turning their heads to the sound of the old truck's rear springs, John Henry was already climbing in the back of the truck. "Ride in back of truck, good for soul. Not like smell of goat herder."

Marty smiled. "See what I mean?"

Leaving the Truck Stop, Marty took the wheel and headed west into the night. In less than an hour, they passed a large sign that read, Welcome to California.

The eastern part of the state was barren with few trees and very little population. North of the Interstate

laid the famous Mojave Desert and
farther to the south was Mexico. As
they drove into the desert, the stars
seemed like diamonds on black velvet.
The night was full of shooting stars
flashing across the horizon.

"Oh, my god!" Amy yelled.

"What?" Marty asked.

"Did you see that shooting star? It
had this bright flame behind it all the
way down." Amy said.

"Babe, you can't just up and scream
like that, not after today." Brett
said.

"I've never seen the sky like this.
It's so beautiful. Sorry I scared you."
She said.

"I guess we're all a little edgy."
Brett said.

As Marty followed the white lines, he
fought hard to stay awake while Brett,
Amy and John Henry slept. Little did he
know the Waitress had mistakenly poured
him unleaded instead of regular. With
no caffeine, his energy began to fade
and with each passing mile, his eyelids
seemed heavier. He couldn't remember
the last time he had been this tired.
He felt as if he had too much to drink
when he hadn't touched a drop.

Shaking his head, Marty slapped his
face and bore down for the long haul.
Less than two hours later, the old
truck began to weave, side to side.

Marty was fast asleep.

The stretch of highway was virtually empty, except for a tractor trailer, now and then.

Most over-the-road trucks along this stretch run at ninety making up for lost time in some city back east. Marty was not only weaving across both lanes, the speedometer read less than 50. He was clueless that another disaster was waiting to happen.

When the truck driver saw the old pickup, he was a half of a mile back and shifted into a lower gear. In his twenty years driving Peterbilts, he had seen plenty of drunks wandering the highways. Each time he savored the opportunity to teach the scumbags a lesson. Barking into his radio, he summoned the Highway Patrol.

"Highway Patrol, what is your emergency?"

"Yea, I'm following a drunk driver in an old red pickup headed west on Interstate 40, about mile marker sixty-four." The truck driver said.

"Sir, do you have a license plate?"

"No, I can't tell, he's all over the road!"

The dispatcher put the trucker driver on hold and summoned the nearest patrol car.

"Dispatch to Unit 40."

"This is 40. Talk to me Linda."

"J.P, we have a possible DUI, mile marker sixty-four, Interstate west bound, driver reported to be in an older red pickup."

"Ok, I'll respond. ETA is twenty minutes."

Hanging up the phone, the truck driver pushed hard on the accelerator and the Semi lurched forward. Now, less than twenty feet behind, the Peterbilt waited to make its move. As the old truck swerved toward the shoulder, the truck driver laid on both horns as he passed.

"Serves you right, you drunk son of a...!"

The four were blasted awake by dual air horns ringing in their ears. Marty jerked the wheel hard left and the old truck swerved back onto the highway. Brett, Amy and John Henry, were terrified as the pickup swerved. Marty settled the truck back into the left hand lane and assumed a 65 mile-per-hour speed.

Wiping his eyes, he gave a forced grin. "No problem, no problem. Everything's all under control." Marty said.

"Marty, what are you doing?" Brett asked.

"He went to sleep that's what." Amy said.

"I just dozed off a little. No big deal." Marty said.

"It's time to switch drivers. Pull over." Brett said.

With an elevation nearing four thousand feet, the Bristol Mountains are in the Mojave Desert of San Bernardino County, California.

Looking for a place to pull over, Marty topped the mountain at 70. They could see the long straight away before them. He began applying the brakes and to his surprise, it went to the floor. He tried a second time and again the brake pedal had no effect. "Damn!" Marty yelled.

The old truck picked up speed and was soon exceeding 80.

"Marty, you're supposed to pull over." Brett said.

"What's wrong?" Amy asked.

"The brakes are out!" Marty yelled.

"What?" Amy asked again but, hearing the first time.

"The brakes are out? Try the emergency." Brett said.

"I did." Marty replied.

As the truck headed toward the bottom of the hill, the speedometer read all of 90 and Amy hugged the dash. "All you had to do was pull over!" She complained.

"Trust me! This is not my idea of a good time!" Marty offered.

Doing 95 and breaking through the darkness at the bottom of the hill, they were too stunned to make a sound. Like three stiff bodies left out in the cold, they were frozen with fear. The truck's headlights exposed certain death as the road curved sharp to the left, impossible to navigate at that speed.

At the last minute, they saw a ray of hope.

"Take the ramp!" Brett yelled.

"I see it!" Marty said.

Marty pulled the wheel to the right and the old truck went up the runaway ramp, which ran nearly parallel to the highway. The ramp was an emergency straightaway more than two hundred feet long filled with six inches of gravel bringing even the heaviest Semi to a dead stop.

As the old truck slowed to a halt halfway up the ramp, they let out a sigh of relief knowing they had cheated death for the third time in less than twenty-four hours. The four sat trembling unable to speak. Amy jumped out and began losing what was left of her last meal. Brett and Marty climbed out and began to decompress. Amy's stomach was swimming like a fish bowl. Brett put a hand on her shoulder.

"You ok?" Brett asked.

"I'll be okay. I just need to lie down for a minute." Amy said.

She sank to her knees and then sat down. Brett looked at John Henry still sitting in the back of the truck. His head was bowed. "John Henry, are you alright?"

"I saw death come and pass." He said.

"The brakes went out." Brett explained.

"If this ramp hadn't shown up, we'd all be fish food right now. Where's your flashlight and I'll take a look?" Marty asked.

Marty crawled under the old truck and found the brake line. From Brett's vantage point, he could see Marty's flashlight follow the brake line from front to rear. "This is weird." He said.

"What else is weird?" Brett asked.

Marty pulled himself out from under the truck and stood next to Brett. "The brake line is fine. No leaks, no brake fluid, nothin."

Amy got up and snuggled under Brett's arm.

"Yea, but, if we lost brake fluid, wouldn't you see where it leaked out?" Brett asked.

"Of course." Marty replied.

"Then, where did it go?" Brett probed.

After more than half an hour trying to decode the mystery of the lost brake fluid, Marty volunteered to walk the five miles to Ludlow, an old ghost town still inhabited with a gas station, restaurant and a repair shop. Walking down the highway, the night was full of sounds that did little to calm his nerves after another near fatal accident. Marty wasn't sure if he was hearing a wolf or coyote. He was thankful the moon was awake as it made him feel he wasn't completely alone. At first, the sound of tires rolling over the highway seemed far away but, kept getting closer as each second passed. When Marty turned around to see who it was, the headlights slowed to a stop while the vehicle let out a short chirp that identified the occupant instantly.

With a jurisdiction of more than half the state, Officer J.P. Smith, a 28 year old school veteran of the California Highway Patrol, turned his spot light on Marty's face blinding both eyes. Stepping out of the Patrol car, he was five foot ten with a pot belly that covered his oversized belt buckle. He had spent most of his years sitting behind the wheel of his cruiser chasing what he hated with obsessed fury, drunk drivers and drug runners. He was not the ideal candidate for any law enforcement academy who usually preferred cadets at least six feet and a body that was not only lean, but could run like a deer. On this night out in the middle of nowhere, he figured he had found the reported DUI, although the only thing missing was the actual pickup the trucker had reported. "Highway Patrol. Stand right where you are and don't you move!"

"Yes, sir." Marty answered.

"Where's your pickup boy?" The officer asked.

"How did you know...?"

"I'll ask the questions. Now where's your pickup?"

"It's back up the road, we.. we ran out of brake fluid."

"Of course you did. Now, who's we?"

"My friends."

"Son, I've had my spot light on the side of the road for near ten miles and I didn't see anything. Now, what'd you do with your truck?"

"We had no brakes, so we took the runaway ramp. I'm on my way to get brake fluid, that's all."

"I see. Have you been drinkin?" He asked.

"Nothin but coffee." Marty said.

"Boy, you drunks are all alike, ever mother son of ya. Stop lying to me. Now, have you been drinkin?"

"All I've had is coffee. I swear."

J.P. started for his breathalyzer kit but was interrupted by the whoosh of a vehicle that blew past the patrol car doing every bit of 90. The sheer force of the wind blew his hair piece just enough to reveal a bald head.

The patrolman had a short temper no one who knew him dared to cross.

Looking at Marty, he barked a quick command. "Get in the car."

Marty stepped to the passenger door of the cruiser and jumped in the front seat, slamming the door. The first thing he noticed was the technology and was amazed that the pot bellied officer could even use any of it. A state of the art radar system, laptop computer, a camera connected to a five inch video screen, and a two-way radio were all ready to make the world a safer place.

"Buckle up son; we're going for a ride!"

Ready for takeoff, Marty clicked the seat belt in place. The officer turned on his lights and slammed the accelerator to the floor throwing Marty against the head rest.

The cruiser was a special edition, one-of a-kind Police Chase Vehicle that sported a five hundred horse power engine that could run at top speeds of over 160 miles per hour. There wasn't anything that Officer J.P. Smith could not catch. He thought. In less than four minutes, they saw the tail lights of the new Cadillac Escalade less than a half mile in front. "I gotcha now, boy!"

J.P. Smith turned on his siren and the Cadillac slowly pulled over.

"What'd you say your name was?"

"Marty... Marty Staggs."

"This may be your lucky day Marty, cause I haven't smelled any booze on ya.

Now, stay right here, don't touch nothin and you just might step out of my cross hairs. You read me?"

"Loud and clear, Sir. "

Marty watched as J.P. walked to the Cadillac SUV and motioned to the driver to step out. As the man got out with his hands in the air, he caught a glimpse of the patrolman in the cruiser's video screen pushing the man up against the SUV. He expected the officer to give the man a ticket but as Marty began to realize this wasn't your average cop.

He watched J.P. open the vehicle's rear door and at gun point, waved the man over to open one of several large duffel bags. Straining his eyes to see what was in the bags, Marty noticed the video screen had a zoom feature and pushed the button to see J.P. holding one of many small plastic bags containing an all white substance. It had to be cocaine, he thought.

After J.P. had placed the nose of his pistol directly in the man's face, Marty saw the drug dealer hand him a brown paper bag. Holding it under one arm, he motioned the drug dealer to pull one of a dozen duffel bags out of the vehicle and placed it on the ground.

As Marty focused on the video screen, it started to beep and began flashing a message that read, Auto Replay. In a panic, he tried to stop the loud noise and pushed the auto replay button by mistake. Realizing his error, he watched as three different video clips showed the rogue cop stopping drug dealers, taking money and a portion of their illegal inventory.

Marty started pressing buttons trying to get the recorder to reset and succeeded just in time to watch J.P motion the man now standing behind the vehicle to kneel down. While shaking his head No, Marty had to look away. What was happening was not only wrong, it was perverted. He had the urge to bolt from the cruiser and run, but, he quickly changed his mind as he watched J.P. tazer the drug dealer who fell against the SUV.

As J.P walked back to the cruiser, the video recorder started beeping again, and Marty desperately started pressing buttons trying to make the noise stop. With the paper bag in one hand and the handle of the duffel bag in the other, J.P. opened the trunk.

Feeling the jolt of the trunk lid shutting behind him, and the video screen still beeping, Marty pushed the restart button just in time as the rogue officer opened the driver side door.

Breathing a sigh of relief, the video was now back in auto record mode as it captured the drug dealer slowly get up and then drive away. In shock from what he had just witnessed, Marty was perspiring. He sat stiff as a board looking straight ahead as J.P. punched the keys on his laptop and issued his report through a sophisticated police network. It was bogus, but it was a report nonetheless.

Punching the key marked SEND, he turned to Marty.

"You alright, boy?" J.P. Smith asked.

"I'm fine. Why wouldn't I be... fine?" Marty asked cautiously.

"You look a little peeked."

"Just relaxin."

"Do you know what's worse than a drug dealer?"

"No, Sir. I surely don't. That would be your area of...."

"It's a drug dealer and a liar all rolled into one. Sometimes, the only choice they give you is the direct approach."

Marty had no idea where this conversation was headed but, he didn't want to find out. He was now ready to get as far away from Officer J.P. Smith as humanly possible. But getting away was not an option. Instead, he figured, he would try to remain on the officer's good side and turned on the charm. "You know, Officer, I'm amazed at the risk you all take in doing your job. Whatever it is they're paying you, it ain't nearly enough."

"No, it's not. Fact is, there are people who clean restrooms who make mor'n we do."

"That's just what I'm saying. So, what do you do in your spare time when you're not putting your life on the line?"

"Well, I like running down to Tijuana on weekends when I can. The whores are all young and pretty."

AS MARTY DID HIS BEST to entertain the officer, Brett, Amy and John Henry tried to pass the time. The sky was still clear and the moonlight was just enough for them to navigate a narrow path on a ridge overlooking the ramp where the truck was parked.

"John Henry, what was it like growing up on the reservation?" Amy asked.

"Great memories. John Henry taught old ways. My father tell great stories. He kept our tribe alive."

"What kind of stories?" She asked.

"When I was young..."

Chapter Twelve

Her name was Chase. She was beautiful and she had a passion for music. That was all I needed to hear.

She also loved horses and had two of her own. They were Appaloosa, a breed of horse that originated with her tribe more than two hundred years before.

Every Sunday we rode out into the desert. Being with her made me forget the ugliness of the past fifteen years. It wasn't too long before I asked her hand in marriage and she became Mrs. Garrett Rivers.

So, I agreed to move out to the Indian reservation as she wasn't really interested in living in town. So, I told her I didn't think I would mind the peace and quiet.

The people on the reservation were mostly up in years and wanted a simple life. They had grandchildren that would come and visit from the towns their sons and daughters had moved.

One night we were sitting under the stars talking and I told her the story of the curse of the James Dean car.

She asked about the day James Dean died and how I got to the crash site.

I explained that I had run out of money for the last stretch to San Francisco.

I was sitting under an aluminum porch in front of an old gas station looking for my next ride when Bill and Sanford pulled up.

I told her they were following James Dean that day and I asked for a ride. They said they were headed to Salinas which was fine by me.

Avoiding the gruesome details of the crash, I told her about what I had found on the road. And, that's when I put it all together.

* * * * * *

MESMERIZED BY John Henry's old Indian stories, Brett and Amy listened in earnest as Marty kept J.P. Smith distracted in conversation about his job, guns and women.

"Well, at least you have your pension." Marty said.

"What do you know about pensions?"

"I just lost mine. You see, pensions are a lot like women. You feed em, you baby em, and then when you lose your job, they leave you at the drop of a hat."

"Ain't it the truth!"

"Yea, women are nothing but a bunch of whores. They use you, take your money, and then like a cold blooded killer, leave you for dead."

Marty's charm was beginning to work its magic. J.P. liked the stranger and began to laugh.

"Sounds like you've met my ex-wife." The officer laughed.

"Sounds like you knew mine. Her name was Wanda May, five foot three and fiery red hair." Marty quipped.

"Boy, you ought to be on late night cable."

Marty's plan to keep J.P. preoccupied in fascinating conversation paid off as the cruiser pulled into the only gas station in Ludlow.

As Marty opened his door, the car radio came alive.

"Unit 40, come in, 40." The dispatcher barked loudly through the speakers.

"This is 40. Talk to me Linda."

"J.P., we have a stolen vehicle headed west on the Interstate. Need an intercept at mile marker ninety seven."

"I'm on it."

"Well, Marty, I got to go. Maybe I'll see you on down the road."

"Happy trails, J.P." Marty closed the passenger door not having the nerve to say it to his face.

"Dipstick!"

The cruiser blew out of the parking lot with lights flashing, leaving a trail of dust.

Pulling his cell phone out of his back pocket, he quickly realized the battery was just about dead. Walking toward the gas station, he knew she would be asleep but, he realized he may not get another chance.

"Marty, it's two in the morning!" Sue moaned.

"I know what time it is." He said.

"Then what's wrong?" She asked.

"Oh, nothin but three accidents in the past nine hours, I'd say everything's Ok."

"What kind of accidents?"

"The kind that's hard to explain, that's what kind. Ever since we left the cemetery, it's been one mystery after another."

"Like what?"

"Like a flash flood nearly pushed us off a cliff. Then, a mudslide nearly covered John Henry's Jeep."

"Who's John Henry?"

"Garrett's second wife's brother. And, third, we lost our brakes coming down a mountain."

"Oh, my God!" Sue said.

"Listen, get a pen so you can write down where we're headed and then.."

Marty's cell phone beeped once letting him know his battery was fast running out of power.

"Damn it! My battery is about dead and I need you to call Sinclair and tell him where to meet up, then we can collect our money."

"Alright, hold on and let me write this down." She said.

As Marty waited, his cell phone beeped again, this time twice. "Come on!" He yelled.

Marty's patience was pushed to the limit as it took Sue nearly a full minute to find a magic marker and a sheet of paper to write on. He just knew his phone would die before she came back. "Sue, hurry up!"

"Ok, I'm ready. Now, where are you going?"

"Call Sinclair and tell him we're headed to the memorial. It's…."

The cell phone beeped three times in a row and then went completely dead. "Damn! Hello! Sue, are you there?"

Marty wanted to throw his phone as far as he could but changed his mind at the last second, knowing he would need it later.

Inside the all night gas station he bought a seven year supply of brake fluid as he was not about to run out again. After a friendly conversation with the station attendant, Marty got him to agree to drop him off as he had to drive east on Interstate 40 anyway.

After waiting nearly an hour, he got his ride back to the old truck.

As Marty walked to the pickup expecting a hero's welcome, he found the passenger door slung wide open and not a soul in sight.

Shouting their names, he hoped they had just gone for a walk.

He said their names as loud as he could.

"Brett, Amy! Where are you?"

Shaking from sheer exhaustion, he lay across the front seat, stretched out and closed his eyes. Without delay his awareness faded and he found himself being handed a large bag of cash by Dugan Sinclair.

Next, he was standing in a Chevy dealership handing over the entire purchase price in cash. The entire staff entered the scene treating him like royalty. The receptionist started giving him a manicure and they poured him a huge glass of champagne. Finally, he pushed the gold key into the ignition. The powerful V8 came to life making a sound sweeter than sex and he took off down the road with the top down. He screeched to a halt next to a gorgeous busty woman by the side of the road and suddenly they were cruising the back roads of Pennsylvania with the beautiful woman stroking his hair. The Corvette came to a sudden stop in a parking space in front of a Motel. The busty blonde applied a second layer of make-up as the desk clerk handed the newlyweds a key to the honeymoon suite not knowing that this particular groom had yet to ask her name. Between hugs and kisses in front of their room and one hand around her waist he kept trying to get the key in the door. He stopped when he heard violent shrieks from inside. Motioning for the beauty to stop the welcomed foreplay, he stood completely still and listened to the sound of animals trying to break out of the room. The crazed screams and loud thumps on the door told him they were not the canine variety.

Finally, the yearnings of the beautiful babe next to him could not be ignored. He was about to kiss her when he was jolted awake.

Face to face with the snout of an ugly beast, Marty watched in horror as it tried to break the back glass of the old truck.

Yelling and jerking backward, he hit his head on the steering wheel.

Marty's eyebrows shot straight up as he realized that he was looking at a Wild Boar obsessed with devouring one hundred and forty-five pounds of human flesh.

The California Wild Boar, closely resembling the domestic hog, is one of the meanest animals known to humankind. Living in groups called Sounders and weighing up to three hundred pounds, the Wild Boar is compact with an oversized head and short legs.

Known by North Americans from the menus of upscale restaurants that serve such fare as Elk or Buffalo, a dozen Wild Boar attacked the old truck. They were dark brown in color and coated from head to hoof with bristles. Between the tusks and the Boar's teeth, there wasn't any hide or bone the animal couldn't tear through. Marty felt a sharp pain in his foot as he looked down and saw one of the beasts had ripped through the heel of his dearly-loved Wolverine's. Thrashing like a fish out of water hoping he could shut the door, but instead his worst nightmare came true. His size-ten boot disappeared into the boar's mouth. A moment later he managed to pull the door shut. He reeled in pain as he examined the red stain on the heel of his naked sock.

Thinking he was finally safe, he turned to see another boar slamming into the back of the pickup, cracking the rear window. Wondering why this nightmare would not end, he turned to see the thief standing on the hood of the pickup gnawing his favorite boot beyond recognition. Like infantryman thrusting a twenty foot log against a mid-evil abutment, a second male boar rammed his ugly snout through the back window, wedging its head in between the frame, not able to move.

Only inches from his face, the beast thrashed and screamed while trying to break through and eat its next meal with Marty as the main course. For what seemed to him as an eternity, Marty and the intruder faced each other.

Seeing the boar working its head further into the cab, Marty kicked its head with his surviving left boot.

"Take that you little bastard!"

For a brief second, the boar stopped and stared straight at him. Not sure whether he was hallucinating, he saw the image of the Medallion in the center of the boar's black eye and for the first time realized why this was happening. Unexpectedly, the boar began retreating, worked its way free and joined the rest of the group as they ran off into the night as quickly as they had appeared.

Completely exhausted, Marty collapsed onto the front seat of the truck when the passenger door flew open.

"Are you Ok?" Brett asked.

"Whoa! You scared the hell out of me." Marty said.

"We didn't sneak up on you, Marty, John Henry just saved your life." Amy said.

"What?" Marty asked in confusion.

"If we hadn't come back when we did, I don't think you'd be making sentences right now." Brett said.

"What are you talking about? My heart feels like it just died a thousand deaths." Marty said.

"John Henry used an old Indian trick and called them off." Amy said.

"Oh, you mean he told a joke only they could get?"

"John Henry hunt the Wild Boar on reservation.

Wild boar very strong."

"John Henry make sound only boar hears." The old Indian said.

"Marty, your foot is bleeding". Amy said,

"I know. One of the beasts tore off my good Wolverines!"

Do you know how long I've had that boot?" Marty asked.

After bandaging Marty's foot and replacing the lost brake fluid, the old truck was back on the interstate.

Looking at the map, Brett figured they had five hours to go if they drove straight through.

Realizing they would have to make one or two more stops and assuming there were no more near accidents or mysterious disasters, they could make the James Dean Memorial by mid-morning.

"I don't know about you two, but I'm starting to think the James Dean curse has found us." Brett said.

Marty listened, but kept completely silent. There was no way he was going to tell them the real reason for all of the near death experiences.

Chapter Thirteen

It wasn't until after my son-in-law's death that I was even told that it had happened. Irene called me and said he died in a wreck in his truck.

I felt that I was the one to blame.

I don't think it would have ever happened if he hadn't gone to pick up what I had so wanted my daughter to have. To me it belonged to my heirs. I wanted Sue to have Noreen's pictures and our wedding album. I suppose I just wanted her to get to know her mother. That's all.

So, before I left Memphis, I had the old trunk I had stored away in San Francisco all those years shipped to her by freight.

Then, it all came together.

One afternoon, I decided to visit Noreen's grave. I had been to see it only once since I had been back to Sedona. I don't know what made me want to see her on that particular day. I guess I just wanted to be there and have some time alone to think.

Sitting next to her headstone, all of a sudden it came to me the cause of all the tragedies and death that had happened and it was very strange that I was still wearing it.

Of course, I thought I knew what it meant when I left Memphis. I even told Doris that I understood the curse of the James Dean car but, I thought at the time that it had to do with anyone who had been near the famous Porsche Spyder. It was then that I realized how misdirected I was when I sat there at her grave, finally understanding the significance of the belt I was wearing.

I remembered the day I wanted a new belt. I had just arrived in Pittsburgh and I had gone to a department store to pick one out.

So, looking through the racks, I finally found one made of black leather. Looking at it, I could see myself wearing it onstage. It was something you just couldn't help but stare at. The only thing I didn't like was that the buckle was too small for the belt. At least that's what I thought. But, I bought it anyway.

On the way home, I remembered the hood emblem from the James Dean car and thought it would make for one very special belt buckle.

I figured the hood emblem would fit on my new belt and if anything, would be an amazing piece of history and best of all, me wearing it.

So, the minute I got home, I went looking for it and, strangely enough, thanked my lucky stars it was still in that old trunk.

It took me a couple of hours but, I found a way to mount the hood emblem to my brand new shiny black leather belt and I started wearing it onstage. From that night on, everything and I mean everything changed.

Sitting there in the cemetery, I finally understood what was driving the curse. Thinking back, it was that very night I put the new belt on that it struck.

We hadn't been onstage thirty minutes and a drunken greedy fool tried to rob the joint. Leonard, the owner of the bar came up behind him and took a beer bottle and smashed it over his head. I thought that served him right. But, we learned the next day that he died of head trauma. I am sure he tried to forget that night.

But, even worse, the curse began to separate good intentions from evil. That's why our drummer was run over by a train. He was one greedy bastard and his death was hard to take, my truck notwithstanding.

It was now so obvious what had eluded me all those years. The hood emblem held the curse and I was its carter.

As I looked straight ahead thinking, I finally came to realize where I was. I was staring right at Noreen's gravestone. And, that's when it occurred to me what I should do with the hood emblem. I understood that I had to put it away someplace where it could no longer do any harm. It wasn't that I thought some of those who died didn't deserve what they got. I believe they did. Yet, it was my family that really mattered and I couldn't see anyone else dying, good or evil. I had had enough.

Taking the belt off, I took the hood emblem and placed it on her gravestone. A few days later, I came back with some mortar and tools and tried my best to make it permanent. No one appreciated the significance of what I had done putting that hood emblem out of harm's way.

From that moment on I tried to put the past behind me. The peace and quiet I was looking for lasted nearly five years when I read that a memorial of James Dean was to be erected near the actual crash site.

I told my second wife why I felt the need to go and help work on the construction of the memorial. It was a way for me to come to grips with the past. To remember, not only James Dean but, more importantly, Bill Hickman and Sanford Roth and how much James Dean meant to them. He was forever their friend and I respected that.

By going to the memorial, I was able to think about what Sanford had told me on the way to Salinas. He said to never stop pursuing your dreams because you never know when your life might be cut short.

I knew he was referring to Dean as there were tears in his eyes. He really loved the young man, his free spirit and his love of life.

My second wife said she understood.

* * * * * *

REACHING BARSTOW, the old truck made a right turn onto Highway 58 that took them past the famous Edwards Air Force Base. Stopping in Bakersfield to eat breakfast and fill up, the four were back on the road in less than an hour turning north onto Interstate 5. Reaching the small town of Lost Hills, Brett turned onto Highway 466, the same Highway on which James Dean was killed nearly fifty years earlier. The landscape was inescapably beautiful even though the rolling hills had far fewer trees than they were used to.

The old pickup followed the straightaway that brought them to the James Dean Memorial. Since this was their final approach, John Henry joined them in the front seat. As they scrunched together in the cab of the truck, their mood began to lighten.

Brett began to smile and put his arm around Amy. She responded and smiled back. "What?" Amy asked.

"We made it! And, in a few minutes we'll finally meet the one and only Garrett Arizona." Brett said.

"Hard to believe we've made it!" Marty said.

From pure exhaustion, Brett started to laugh. Then, little by little they all began to laugh.

Marty flapped him wings like a bird and they all began to roar.

IN ITS PRESENT STATE, the James Dean Memorial was only a framed structure and on this day, a mixed crew of about twenty volunteers covered the small construction site like ants on an ant hill.

Approaching the memorial from the opposite direction, a black Peterbilt with a forty-five foot trailer and seventy thousand pounds of cargo was behind schedule. As it passed the new construction site, an old Buick pulled into the road right in front of the Semi. The driver slammed on his brakes, causing the tires to smoke.

Jackknifed, the Semi slid sideways down the road toward the old truck. Still screaming with laughter, the four suddenly saw a solid wall of a Tractor Trailer coming right at them. There was no escape as their laughter now turned into screams of horror.

Simultaneously, they ducked down into the floorboard as the front end of the pickup dove under the Trailer, the cab was decapitated. Coming out the other side, the headless pickup spun out of control heading directly toward the Memorial. It came to rest in the front parking area while the Semi came to a halt one hundred yards down the road.

The crew, motionless as they watched the wreck in progress, climbed down from the construction site and ran over to see if they could help. A crowd of workers looked at the four jammed into the bottom of the cab. "Are you okay?" Someone said.

"Is this place of spirit world?" John Henry asked.

"No. It's California."

As the four were helped out, Brett reached for Amy and wrapped his arms around her, holding her tight. "Brett, I was so scared." Amy said.

"It's okay. We're finally here." Brett reassured her.

"Does anyone need an ambulance?" Another worker asked.

"I don't think so. Marty, are you Ok?" Brett asked.

"Oh, man, what a nightmare!" He said.

As they looked each other over, a tall man walked through the crowd toward them.

He was an older and wiser version of the twenty year old they had seen in the picture with Bill Hickman.

John Henry recognized him. "Garrett!"

"John Henry. What are you doing here?" Garrett Arizona asked.

"We come to see you." He replied.

"Garrett, this is your Grandson Brett. Girlfriend Amy and, Uncle Marty."

Garrett walked over to Brett and put his hand out and shook it. "Hello Brett. Amy. Marty. What are the four of you doing out here?" He asked.

"Granddad, I…, I found the letters you wrote and not knowing if you were still alive, we set out to find you."

"Well, I'm mighty impressed, to say the least. Looks like you just about got yourself killed in the process."

"We've had few close calls lately." Brett replied.

"Yeah, it's been one accident after another ever since we left Sedona. The cemetery to be exact." Amy said.

"You don't say." Garrett inquired.

As Garrett stood back and looked at them with suspicion, Marty began to cower. He grimaced like a young child about to be punished. "I, I can explain. It's not how you think."

"Explain what?" Amy asked.

"What are you saying, Marty?" Brett asked.

"There's this Medallion and, and there's a reward, see? And, me and Sue thought there'd be no harm in…

Ok! It was there! Right out in the open. And, and, it was beggin! Beggin for me to cash it in!"

"Let me guess. You took the Medallion from the cemetery." Garrett said.

"It's worth a lot of money!"

As Marty cowered, a man walked up and interrupted his confession.

"Excuse me! I've believe that piece of history is already spoken for."

Turning their heads, they watched the sharply dressed man and his four body guards approach.

"And, who sir might you be?" Garrett asked.

"Sinclair. Dugan Sinclair, at your service.

If you must know, I've already made arrangements with Mr. Staggs to collect the Medallion. Now, it is simply a matter of money."

"You're assuming that it's his to sell." Garrett replied.

"Mr. Arizona, the Medallion was part of the Porsche Spider owned by the late James Dean. I have purchased that automobile and I am within my rights to demand its return.

However, I have generously agreed to a reward."

"It's not yours yet, you greedy son of a...banker." Marty protested.

As Marty pulled the Medallion out of his bag, Brett and Amy recoiled. Holding it up, the sun caused it to glow with patterns of light that shown through it. Inside, images of all things tortured in Hell were visible.

"Mr. Sinclair, this piece of Hades has been with me for more than fifty years and has caused nothing but misery and pain. Even if you can prove you own it, there's no way I could let you have it, knowing it would be the cause of your untimely death." Garrett said.

Dugan Sinclair smiled. He had read about the so called curse of the James Dean car but, never believed it to be true. "Mr. Arizona, please spare me the tales of global calamity. I know about the curse and that was nearly fifty years ago."

"More than enough people have died, Mr. Sinclair. There's no need for you to be on that list." Garrett said.

"Look around, Mr. Arizona, these men are here to protect me and my interests. And, protect it they will!"

Marty spoke up. "Mr. Sinclair, I'm the one who found the Medallion and I'm the one that needs the money."

"Good choice, Mr. Staggs." Dugan Sinclair said. "Let's do some business, shall we?"

"I want five hundred thousand and not a penny less!" Marty said.

"That is what I was prepared to offer. You can come with me and count it yourself, Mr. Staggs."

Brett and Amy could not believe what they were hearing. "What are you doing, Marty?" Amy asked.

"Marty, you don't want to do this." Brett said.

"I didn't come all this way to leave empty handed." Marty replied.

"Let's go, Mr. Staggs. I've instructed my banker to meet us in Salinas. After it's verified, the money is all yours."

With that, Dugan Sinclair directed Marty to a black Lincoln. After climbing in, the shiny black car roared out of the parking lot, leaving Brett and Amy in utter shock.

Neither could believe that Marty could be so greedy and foolish after what they had all been through.

To them, it was more than a dream, they were living a nightmare.

"Your Uncle, has he always been this way, impetuous and fool hardy to boot?" Garrett asked.

"I thought I knew him but, I guess I really didn't." Brett said.

"He was just laid off from his job." Amy offered. "I guess he needed the money."

"That Medallion doesn't take kindly to greed. It took me many years to figure that out. I hope he survives it." Garrett said.

Before they could say another word, the brakes of the black Lincoln went out and the car rammed into a light pole, exploding into a fiery ball of destruction.

"Oh, my god! Marty!" Amy yelled.

Climbing into Garrett's truck, the four drove toward the fiery crash, knowing what it all meant. As they approached, they were forced to stop, blinded by the flames.

After nearly a minute and not believing their eyes, the silhouette of a dark figure appeared against the backdrop of the inferno.

It was Marty.

He was carrying a small silver briefcase.

Jumping out of the truck, the four ran toward him.

"Marty, we thought!" Amy started.

"You're not dead!" Brett exclaimed.

"Of course I'm not dead."

"Spirits say you live still."

"Awe, I missed you guys. I couldn't go through with it so I gave him the Medallion and he let me out." Marty said.

"What's that?" Brett asked.

"It's what I call freedom."

Marty opened the briefcase revealing neatly wrapped bundles of one hundred dollar bills.

As they stood in disbelief, Garrett smiled to himself and slapped John Henry on the back. Amy threw her arms around Brett.

Looking at the money, Marty laughed out loud as he explained what happened.

"We closed out the transaction." Then, Marty looked over his shoulder at the smoldering black Lincoln.

"But, not to his satisfaction."

Overcome with emotion, Amy ran over to Marty and wrapped her arms around him.

"Marty, you are a good man after all."

"You didn't think I'd let you go to Paris without me, did ya?" He asked.

"You're not going to Paris, you goat herder." Amy cried.

She kissed him on the cheek and they all piled into the truck.

Sitting in front, Garrett and Brett had a lifetime to catch up on.

Marty sat in the back with Amy and John Henry.

ACROSS THE ROAD, a California Highway Patrol car pulled up, lights flashing.

Crawling out of the cruiser, J.P. Smith walked toward the wreckage.

As the truck pulled away, Marty ducked down as he saw the overweight patrolman stop, bend down and pick up a shiny piece of metal. He looked it over carefully and without another thought, put it into his pocket.

Staring into nowhere as the truck drove away, a smile crept across Marty's face as he looked into the future.

It was….. The Medallion.

Order The Audio Movie!

If you enjoyed Mystery of The Medallion in paperback, you have to experience the sounds of the full length audio version. Listen as Marty, Brett and Amy track down Garrett Arizona and discover the Mystery of The Medallion! It's no ordinary audio book, it's an Audio Movie!

To order, visit;

www.Interskillmedia.com
and choose the 'Products' icon.

To receive a 50% discount on the Audio Movie, use the correct promotional code when ordering online. The code is the license plate number of Garrett Arizona's wrecked pickup truck which was located in the salvage yard.

Other Paperback Titles & Audio Movies Available:

Lost Nation by Joshua Ground

An Army of Idiots by Austin Teutsch

Hindsight by Susan Lynn Perry

Audio Movie
The Bet by L.A. Hoyt, Jeff Edwards, Christina Johnson, Jennifer MacDonald and Gary Huff

Order The Music of
Brett Staggs!

The music of Brett Staggs is available
at Itunes and InterSkillMedia.com

Mystery of The Medallion
Soundtrack

The Puzzle

Gamblin' Man

This Cold Town

Let's Go Out Tonight

Meet Me At The Restaurant

If You're Sellin' (I'm Buyin')

Electric Heart

Saddleback Farm

I Am Here For You

Wake Me Up!

To order, visit;

www.Interskillmedia.com/buy